PRAISE FOR *OLD MEN*

As a convert to the Catholic Chu
I've frequently struggled with
Saints—sure, I have great respect and reverence for them, but would I
have said we were good friends? Perhaps not. And despite being
beyond blessed as a Dominican Sister of St. Joseph to be under his
patronage, I always struggled most of all in getting to know St. Joseph
as a flesh-and-blood person. Seeing him through Katie's eyes (as well
as Razim's in DO CARPENTERS DREAM OF WOODEN SHEEP?) has had a
beautiful and unexpected impact on my own relationship with him
and—finally—I've found a friend and spiritual father in St. Joseph!

SR. M. CATHERINE BLOOM, OP

How can St. Joseph help a modern teenage girl? The saints aren't dis-
tant in "Old Men Don't Walk To Egypt;" this story provides a relatable
look at high school life that resonates with anyone who has struggled
with relationships, expectations, and faith. You might not cry like I did,
but there's a takeaway for everyone about friendship, romance, and
honesty. I can't wait to share this story with others. Ite ad Joseph.

LISA THEUS

Corinna Turner has done it again! This talented author really has
perfected the craft of creating memorable faith-filled stories full of
relatable characters dealing with societal hot-topics. Teens are
growing up in a world with increasingly more dangerous societal
expectations. It is critical that we arm them with role models and
strategies to deal with these issues from a Catholic perspective, and
this is what Turner does so expertly with this story. As the main
character learns more about St. Joseph for a school project, she
receives the insight and inspiration that help her deal with her own
problems. What a powerful book for teens.

LESLEA WAHL, author of the Blindside series

Engaging characters and realistic scenarios make this story of faith,
grace and the intercession of St. Joseph very accessible
to young people.

SR. TERESA CARDINEZ, OP

ALSO BY CORINNA TURNER:

† Coming Soon
* Awarded the Catholic Writers Guild *Seal of Approval*

Old Men Don't Walk to Egypt

FRIENDS IN HIGH PLACES 2: SAINT JOSEPH

CORINNA TURNER

unSeen

CONTENTS

CHAPTER 1

MONDAY

"Hey, Katie." Shaun's eyes flick up and down me as I stop beside him in the quiet corridor, and he smiles, his arm slipping around my shoulders possessively. The ear loops of his face mask show from one trouser pocket and I slip mine off as well.

Everyone else is still in the cafeteria, eating, but with the Covid rules about class 'bubbles' this is the only time Shaun and I can meet. Even after two weeks I can still hardly believe that he actually wants me for his girlfriend! I mean, he's gorgeous, he's a fantastic rugby player, and he's two years older than me!

"Did you hear about the flash woodworking competition?" I ask him. Woodworking's not really my thing, but I have such a good idea. I'm bursting to tell him.

"Yep." He runs a hand through his hair, tousling it

in a way that really suits him. "We won't be able to hang out in the park much this week; I've got to make the winning entry."

We only have one week to make our pieces and submit them. Deadline is next Monday. It's open to all four of the oldest year groups.

"I was, uh, I was thinking of entering too."

He raises his eyes from the region of my chest to glance at my face. "You?"

"Yeah. I have this fantastic idea. I know I'm not that great at woodworking but I thought maybe you could"—at the way he's frowning I swallow 'help a little' and finish lamely— "give me a few pointers?"

He's really scowling now. "Katie, I just told you I'm entering. Why would you put me in such an awkward position? Asking me to help you? That would just be silly."

"I didn't mean..." I speak quickly, my heart pounding. "I mean, I'm so..." *So rubbish at woodwork that even with your help I'm hardly going to be competition and I am your girlfriend...* But I shut up. "No, you're right. It was silly. Forget it."

He slides his arm down to my waist, lowering his head to nuzzle my cheek, but hurt and uncertainty still slosh in my stomach. I pull my phone out and ease away from him to get enough elbow room to check it.

"Why do you always do that?" His voice is sharp.

2

"Do what?"

"Pull away and check your phone?"

"I...I thought I heard a text alert." It's a lie, but he's looking so angry and hurt. Yet he's always checking his own phone, even if I'm speaking.

"Whatever."

I start to put the phone away but he pulls me right against him and I've drawn back before I can think. Trying to cover it up, I raise my phone again, but he grabs my wrist.

"Why don't you just put that thing away?"

"Ow! Shaun!"

"Why don't *you* get your hands off her?" The quiet voice speaks from only feet away and we both spin around. Surely I'm not *hoping* for a teacher? We're both maskless and in violation of the bubble rule...

...Aw, heck. Worse. It's a boy from my year, Daniel—bald and gaunt and pale-faced. I barely know him. When I arrived at the beginning of the school year he seemed like a quiet, slightly nerdy boy who stuck with his group of friends and didn't make any waves, but then about half-way through the term he started getting in bully's faces like he had a death wish, then he disappeared—having chemo, apparently. Some of the meaner kids were betting on whether he was going to die. He reappeared during the brief period schools were open after Christmas—bald and skeletal—then during the spring Lockdown there were rumors he was having more chemo. And now he's back again. Still bald, so I guess the rumors were correct.

Alive, though. And apparently still with a death wish, if he's getting in the face of my eighteen-year-old rugby player boyfriend.

"*What did you say?*" Shaun demands.

"You shouldn't be grabbing her like that."

"She's *my* girlfriend, baldie." Shaun towers over skinny Daniel, who just stares up at him, unmoved. Guess anyone who beats up the kid with leukemia will probably get expelled and he knows it.

"All the more reason," he says calmly.

Shaun looks like he's about to flatten Daniel, expulsion or not, so I say quickly, "Why are you interfering, Daniel? Shaun wasn't doing anything."

"Do you know this sack of bones?" demands Shaun. "Isn't this the Jesus-freak with cancer?"

"He's in my year, that's—" But before I can say 'all' Shaun's spun around and marched off.

"Thanks for nothing," I snap at Daniel.

"You're welcome," he says dryly.

"Freak!"

He shrugs. I pull out my mask and turn to go.

"Oh, Katie."

"What?"

"How are you doing with Mrs. Gunnings' saint

4

research project?"

"Haven't even chosen a saint yet...." Just in time, I bite off, 'not that it's any of your business.' I mean, he's into that sort of thing, right? If he has to butt in like this, he can at least help me. "Got any tips?"

"Saint Joseph would be a good one, I reckon."

"Right." If he thinks Saint Joseph's easy to research, that'll do for me.

I head a few steps down the corridor, but pause when I see Daniel's handsome friend Razim striding towards us. Taller and broader-shouldered than Daniel, his skin is a warm brown shade, although—alas—gone is the glossy black hair with the adorable wave. He shaved it off a couple of weeks ago in some mad act of solidarity with Daniel. His older brother didn't know he'd done it until he saw him in school and they had a fight right there in the cafeteria. Seemed an overreaction on his brother's part. Much as I mourn the hair, it was a sweet thing to do.

Razim is nice-looking, even without it. I think he's quite good at football. But he doesn't seem to know I exist and, anyway, Shaun's even more handsome. And on the rugby team. And older. My friends just can't believe I'm Shaun's girlfriend, any more than I can.

Razim's vague nod towards me acknowledges that we're in the same year group, but he doesn't seem to realize I was just talking to Daniel because he goes straight up to him without looking at me again.

"Why are you hauling that around yourself, man?" Razim snags the rucksack from Daniel's shoulder and swings it onto his own back. "You'll wear yourself out and then your mum will make you stay home. Come and sit down. Where did you go, anyway?"

"I just wanted to check something out."

I think from the way his eyes crinkle above his mask that Daniel smiles at me, then he allows his friend to herd him away.

I stare after him. Check something out? Did he follow me? Why would he do that?

Ignoring the little voice that says Daniel was nearby when Shaun shouted—that is, raised his voice a bit— last week, I slip my mask on and rub my wrist. Shaun doesn't know his own strength, that's all. Daniel should keep his nose out of other people's business.

CHAPTER 2

MONDAY

When I get home and open my laptop, the webpage with the plans for my woodworking idea is there on the screen. But I won't be entering now, right? Shaun's made it clear he won't help and—well, maybe it *would* be silly for us both to enter. But...

I gaze at the plans. Lack of experience or not, I can see it, finished, in my head. But can I really do it on my own?

Firmly, I open a new webpage. The saint project is also due next Monday; I've got to at least make a start on it. Everything rests on our class work, right now. No exams—*thanks, Covid*—but that means our teachers will be deciding our grades.

Saint Joseph. Husband of Mary, Jesus's mother, right? My mum used to drag me to Mass every Sunday, until...

I scowl at the screen as I type in the saint's name, but I can't stop my brain finishing the sentence. Until she found out what was going on with Dad's boss and divorced him. We don't go to Mass, now, though I did sneak into a Christmas Mass. It just didn't seem like Christmas the year before, when I didn't go. And with everything that happened in 2020...well, I didn't tell my mum, but I went.

Hey, Daniel was right, there's loads of stuff on Saint Joseph. I click a likely-looking entry.

The picture shows a handsome young man who looks a bit like a slightly older version of Razim, standing beside what's clearly Mary and baby Jesus. I thought Saint Joseph was an old guy? I scan the text.

Saint Joseph of Nazareth, also known as Saint Joseph the Carpenter... Oh, of *course*! He was a carpenter! Is this, like, a sign from God or the universe that I should enter that competition? Somehow, after what happened with Shaun, I want to even more, even though at the same time I'm afraid it will annoy him.

I skim down the article even further. What's this? Saint Joseph is believed to have built a mysterious spiral staircase for a bunch of nuns in America? There's even a movie about it. Okay, that is *weird*. Still...carpentry, huh?

"Okay, I'm gonna do it," I tell the picture of the saint on the screen. "I'm gonna enter! But you may need

8

to help me!"

Quickly, I note down a list of Saint Joseph's most important titles for my project. What should I focus on? Everyone will know his story already—they've heard it in every nativity play since nursery. I haven't been to Mass for three years—except Christmas—and I still know it backwards.

Let's see, Joseph is engaged to Mary, she gets pregnant by the Holy Spirit, Joseph is too nice to want her to be stoned so he intends to divorce her quietly, thus sparing her life. But the angel comes in his sleep and tells him it was the Holy Spirit knocked her up and that he should marry her anyway, so he does—which, now that I really think about it, shows quite some trust for the angel. Or maybe God.

Then they have to go to Bethlehem for the census at just the wrong time and poor Mary ends up giving birth to Jesus in a stable. King Herod wants to kill Jesus but the angel warns Joseph and he takes Mary and Jesus to Egypt for a while. That's about it, right?

Oh, maybe not. Reading through the article more slowly, I realize I've missed a few bits out. Eight days after he was born, the baby had to be circumcised— *ouch*—and Joseph named him Jesus, as the angel had told him too. By naming him, he took legal responsibility for him under Jewish law. Like an adoption, though everyone else assumed Joseph was

Jesus's biological father. Six weeks after the birth, they also had to go to Jerusalem to make an offering in the temple. That was called the 'Presentation.'

But what was the offering *for*? Okay, it says here... In ancient Judaism every firstborn—whether person or domestic animal or cultivated plant—belonged to God. 'Firstborn' animals or plants were given to him in sacrifice, but with people, an animal sacrifice was substituted, for obvious reasons! Rich people would sacrifice more, but the poor could just sacrifice a pair of turtledoves or two young pigeons. Joseph must have been poor, because that's what he offered for Jesus.

Sacrificing things like that seems odd, though I vaguely remember from the Old Testament that it was really important. Why would you do that? Isn't that like having a business transaction with God? I'll give you this, if you give me that?

Heat rises to my cheeks and I shift on my chair. Okay, maybe I understand it better than I thought. When everything was going supernova between Mum and Dad, I remember offering God all sorts of things if He'd only fix it. I offered to do stuff for Him; I offered Him my possessions...

But apparently He didn't want any of it, because Mum divorced Dad anyway. And if only it had ended there. I don't think Mum even realizes that I know the rest, but, I mean, there's Google, right? We moved to

10

another town — twice — not another planet...

It still doesn't explain why Dad hasn't called me or written to me once in the last three years. Nothing explains that. Except that he doesn't care anymore.

I try to push the thoughts out of my head. Huh, the article's answering my question. Apparently Old Testament sacrifices were to do with covenants, which are about a relationship, as opposed to contracts, which are just a business deal. But they still sacrificed despite having that 'covenant' relationship with God, because of the Old Law and God's justice requiring it. But Jesus made Himself into, like, the sacrifice to end all sacrifices and paid for everything on our behalf, all at once. So we don't have to sacrifice anymore.

I frown at the screen. Justice, huh? And Jesus paid everything. It makes a kind of sense, though I'm betting I'm missing a lot. Not that I'm even sure about God, anymore, really.

My phone buzzes and I scrabble for it frantically. Is it Shaun? Is he mad about Daniel interfering like that? But it's Elena, telling me the date concerts may be resuming. I text back, trying to sound enthusiastic, and go back to my researching.

I wind Mum up at dinner grabbing my phone every time it buzzes, but I can't help it. I'm so worried Daniel's blown it with me and Shaun. Meddling weirdo. But by the time I'm back at my computer Shaun still hasn't contacted me. Should I text him? But I don't want to make him mad. Madder.

I click on another Saint Joseph link instead. A letter by the pope. That could be useful. I skim through the first part.

Okay, so we're in the 'Year of Saint Joseph' right now. I didn't even know. Yep, I'm getting the feeling Saint Joseph is important. Apparently Blessed Pius IX declared him "Patron of the Catholic Church," Venerable Pius XII named him "Patron of Workers" and Saint John Paul II as "Guardian of the Redeemer." And he's universally invoked as the "patron of a happy death."

I stare at the last bit, then shake my head. That really is too weird. What's happy about dying? I scroll down for a while longer, before closing my file of Saint Joseph notes and plowing through my Mathematics homework, then watching an episode of my favorite soap.

I'm about to get ready for bed when my phone buzzes.

I grab it for the hundredth time.

Shaun. Every muscle tenses as I tap and read the message.

Hi gorgeous. What u doing?

My stomach unclenches. He's not mad about earlier. I'd a horrible feeling, when he stormed off like that, that he was mad at me as well as Daniel, even though that made no sense. But he's not.

I text back:

About to shower & bed. U?

The reply soon pops up.

Just finished working out.

He's attached a photo of his rock-hard abs, glistening with sweat. Phew! He is toned. I feel a little breathless as I text back:

Not bad. ;)

His reply appears almost at once:

How about a sexy pic?

CHAPTER 3

MONDAY

When I finally get into bed I can't hold it in anymore. I lie, hugging my pillow, and sob. What should I have done or not have done? I don't even know.

I mean, I knew what sort of 'sexy pic' Shaun was hoping for. Of course I did. But I just… I mean, we've only been dating two weeks, for one thing. And even if we'd been going out longer…I'm not comfortable with that.

But I couldn't bear to say no, either. Especially after what happened earlier. So after I had my shower I put on some discrete makeup and then took a picture with my towel wrapped around me, trying for a sexy coquettish look to make up for the fact he couldn't really see anything. And I sent it to him.

I figured he'll see as much if I ever wear a strapless dress to a party—not that Mum will buy me one of those. So I thought it didn't matter. But once I'd pressed 'send' I just felt…dirty.

It doesn't make *sense*, but it felt *horrible*. Like I'd cheapened myself. I mean, he couldn't really *see* anything, right?

He didn't even reply for ages. I was far too strung-up to go to bed. And then, finally:

Call that a sexy pic?

And now I'm crying. My chest is all tight and I feel like every shadow in the room is squeezing in on me. Oppressed. That's how I feel. Like, if there is a devil, he's laughing all around me.

I sent that photo when I really didn't want to, and it was all for nothing.

Yeah, the devil's laughing. I can feel him. I pull the covers over myself and go back to hugging my pillow, shaking.

Maybe it's just too late and I'm too tired and I'm freaking out after a stressful day, but it really feels like there's something in the room, about to attack me. Maybe already attacking, unseen. And it's scaring me.

Terror of demons…

What? Hang on, I read that phrase tonight. It was on the list of titles of Saint Joseph. Terror of Demons. Does that mean…?

"Saint Joseph, Terror of Demons, pray for me," I whisper. Weren't those the words?

The feeling of oppression eases. Emboldened, I throw back the duvet, sit up straight and speak full-volume into the darkness. "Saint Joseph, Terror of Demons, pray for me!"

And the feeling's gone. Completely. Just like that.

Huh. *Thanks, Saint Jo.*

Guess Daniel gives better tips than I thought.

It's too hot for a cloak, but I'm wearing one anyway. I try to keep it gathered close around me as I hurry back from the marketplace, the heavily-laden wicker basket bashing my knees. It's late, but it's pleasanter to shop once most of the women of Nazareth have been and gone. It doesn't matter to me if they talk, of course, but gossip harms them, and I prefer not to be the cause.

The sun is dropping in the sky as I trudge towards Joseph's house. I'm close enough that I stop worrying about the cloak. The neighbors see my rounded belly every time I go to draw water—they barely even whisper anymore. Joseph often comes to the market with me, but travelers arrived at the door with a broken cartwheel just as I was setting off.

I'm about to turn the final corner to Joseph's street—my street, now—when a man steps from a doorway and catches hold of my arm.

"Well, hello, if it isn't the carpenter's hussy, out alone.

16

Why don't you step inside for some wine?"

I pull my arm free and try to go on past, refusing to reply. A woman alone does not speak to a man in public, as he well knows.

But he grabs me again, pulling me towards the house. "Come, hussy, your husband will never know. Might not care, either. They reckon that babe may not even be his, but he was too soft-hearted a fool to see your pretty face smashed by the stones you so rightly deserve."

I pull free again. I refuse to speak to him! But he still won't let me past. Until a large hand settles on his shoulder.

"Hiram, you're in my wife's way. Please step aside." At the deep slow voice and the strength of that grip on his shoulder, Hiram's face pales.

"Oh...sorry, Joseph. Didn't see her there." He pulls free of Joseph's hand with even more difficulty than I pulled free of his and slides back into his house like the snake he reminds me of.

"Let me have that." Joseph takes the heavy basket from me and slips a protective arm around my shoulders, leading me away. "I should have come with you, broken wheel or not." Self-reproach fills his voice.

"Of course not. Stranded travelers must come first. Anyway, your timing was excellent. Hiram won't bother me again, and he's the only one likely to. Did you not see the way he bolted?"

Joseph chuckles, deep and warm. "Indeed I did."

17

I wake and lie for a while, remembering a strong arm around me, like a wall of warmth and safety, and a slow, deep laugh. Shaun's never made me feel like that. Not yet, anyway. Maybe he will, someday—but it's hard to imagine. Mary was a lucky woman.

CHAPTER 4

TUESDAY

My steps are heavy as I head for the quiet corridor where Shaun will be waiting. What will he say? I wish last night hadn't happened. I was so happy about having Shaun for a boyfriend, but now I just feel awkward.

He comes towards me with a smile, though, and slips his arm around me the way he always does, holding me a fraction too tight. Yeah, he doesn't know his own strength. All those muscles.

"You okay, Katie?"

Ignoring the little voice that says Joseph didn't hold me too tight when I was Mary—and wouldn't anyone who heard me thinking that sentence think I was mad!—I quickly drag a smile onto my face. "Yeah, fine. Just a little tired. How's your woodworking entry going?"

I don't have to say anything for a while, other than nod and smile as he tells me all about what he calls 'the winning entry.' It does sound cool. He really has a lot of different talents.

But then he's lowering his face, his cheek brushing mine. "That pic was so 'good little Catholic schoolgirl.' Made me really hot."

What? That's not what he said last night!

His lips brush against my cheek. How can I get out of this? What? Don't I want him to kiss me? Haven't I been fantasizing about it after that tiny peck last week? But…

I realize I've turned my head slightly, avoiding full contact, and he's gone very tense. But when he speaks his voice is still soft, seductive, friendly… "Yes, a very sexy picture. A good job your mum will never see it, isn't it? She might think it was the tip of the iceberg."

What? Why is he mentioning my mum? He's not…*surely* he's not hinting that…that he would show it to her? Of course not! It's horrible of me to even think that. Heck, if my mum saw that… I'm getting goose bumps at the thought.

I know it's not what he means, of course it's not. But when he swoops for my lips again I try very hard to stay still and enjoy the kiss. Not *just in case*, of course. Just…just *because*.

+

I walk blindly down the corridors, avoiding the cafeteria where my friends will look at me with envious eyes and demand every detail. My throat feels so tight, like I could cry, but I've just had my first proper kiss. I should be ecstatic. Instead, that dirty feeling from last night grips me worse than ever.

I really feel like I might cry. I've got to get out of sight. My year group classroom is coming up, so I open the door and slip inside. Only as I close the door behind me do I realize there's someone in here.

Daniel sits at a desk with a lunchbox in front of him, his mask lying discarded, and from the second lunchbox nearby, someone else has been in here recently. I back up, reaching for the doorknob.

"It's okay," says Daniel, smiling at me over the top of a brown bread sandwich with vast quantities of greenery sticking out of it. "My immunity's not all the way back up yet, so I'm supposed to avoid everyone when they've got their masks off eating. But you're just one person, so you don't have to go."

I don't want to cry in front of Daniel, but I don't really want to go back out into the corridor either. Since Daniel's here, I'll probably manage not to break down. I hope. I sink into a chair, not too close since I've just realized I've forgotten to put my mask back on. Heck, is my lipstick smeared? Now I'm embarrassed.

With a rather dutiful air, Daniel takes another bite

21

of his sandwich and chews steadily, seeming to notice nothing odd about my face.

Groping for something to say, I blurt, "Are you really..." *dying*, is what I mean, but I trail off. How can I ask him that, he'll think me ghoulish? But he's looking at me inquiringly so, feeling committed, I stutter, "really, uh, are you really, um, going to, uh...?"

Understanding flashes across his face. "Oh, die?" he says calmly. "Well..." He chews and swallows the last of his bite... "Yes. We all die. Didn't you get the memo?"

A cold prickle shoots up my spine. I mean, I know that, of course, but...it's not something I really *think* about.

Daniel's smiling, though, so he doesn't seem offended by my question. He goes on, "Am I going to do it quite a while before you probably do? Maybe. It's not really clear, yet. The latest test results seem quite good so the short-term long-term is looking hopeful, if that makes any sense."

How can he be so calm? "Aren't you scared?" Heck, I can't ask him that. I barely know him.

But he just nods. "Sometimes, yes. But I try not to be. I mean, it's quite exciting, when you really think about."

Exciting? Is he nuts?

He sees my expression and his smile widens. "I

mean, think how exciting it would be to meet a famous athlete or a celebrity or, I dunno, the queen? And then think about meeting God Himself, the Creator, who is love and truth and beauty beyond anything we can possibly grasp. Isn't that exciting? Or shouldn't it be?"

When I stare at him, unable to respond, he adds, "Don't get me wrong, I hope it won't happen just yet — it would be so hard on my parents." The sadness in his eyes makes my stomach clench. "And I do really like being alive. But" — his smile comes back — "it really is up to God, y'know?"

Desperately, I rack my brains for a way to change the subject. "So, uh, it turns out it's the Year of Saint Joseph. D'you think everyone will have chosen him?"

He shakes his head. "Doubt many people know."

"You're not doing him?"

"No. I'm doing Blessed Carlo Acutis. Did you know he actually knew he was going to die young? When he was a small boy he predicted the cause of his death exactly, and only a few months before he died he predicted his weight at the time of his death, also exactly. It's on video."

Cold prickles run up my spine. "Great." I speak shortly, but I can't help it. "Do you *ever* talk about anything cheerful?"

"Hey, you brought up death, not me."

Heck, does he have to keep saying the word? He's

23

freaking me out with his attitude. I could just leave, but even freaky Daniel is better than running into Sh... that is, wandering around aimlessly.

"Uh, I was puzzled by one thing." My brain throws up a useful question. "I thought Saint Joseph was an old guy, but in the picture I found online he was young." And in my dream, too...

Daniel brightens. "Yeah, that's really interesting. For a long time there was this tradition that he was old, out of, like, this misguided attempt to protect Our Lady's virtue. But gradually saints and scholars started pointing out that, actually, he was probably young, because Jewish marriages at the time were usually between people well-matched in age."

"But they didn't have a normal marriage, right? Because Mary was always a virgin?"

"Yeah." He nods. "A lot of people think Joseph was, too. After all, God would've given Mary a wonderful man who was generous and virtuous and self-controlled, not one who was simply too old to be interested. But there *was* this theory that older men might have sometimes married women who'd consecrated themselves in the temple as virgins, just to act as protectors to them. But the fact is there's no actual evidence how old Saint Joseph was except what is in scripture. And as a famous nun called Mother Angelica pointed out, old men don't walk to Egypt."

He bites into his sandwich as though this statement confirms everything he's just said.

"Uh...?"

"Oh." He chews quickly and swallows. "Well, think about the evidence from scripture—when Jesus and Mary are in danger, Joseph flees with them to Egypt. Now, Mary had a donkey to ride, but Joseph walked every step of the way. And also from Nazareth to Bethlehem—that's at least eighty miles on foot. And a similar distance from Nazareth to Jerusalem at least once a year, maybe even three times a year. That's a heck of a lot of walking. He must have been young or, at very least, not old-old."

"I guess that makes sense."

I eye Daniel as he chews resignedly at another mouthful of super-healthy sandwich. For some reason I want to open my mouth and tell him about what happened with Shaun just now. It's crazy, I barely know him, and what I was thinking about Shaun is so unfair. I can't go slandering my boyfriend to a weirdo stranger.

But my mouth really wants to spill the words out. I'm not sure if I can stop myself. In fact...I'm drawing a deep breath...my lips are parting...

The door opens and I start violently, my heart pounding.

It's not Shaun, of course, it's Razim. He sinks into

the chair in front of the other lunchbox, depositing a handful of snacks onto the desk in front of him, then slips his mask off, tossing it aside. Giving me a polite smile, he leans over to dump a few items in front of Daniel, who drops the remains of the sandwich back into his lunchbox and rips open a chocolate bar.

"Ah, thanks, Raz. You're a lifesaver."

Razim shoots a sympathetic look from the sandwich to Daniel. "Your mum is really overdoing it with the healthy eating."

"Yeah, well, I'm simply too nice to go pointing out that I probably really might as well eat just as many snacks and unhealthy things as I like."

I stare at him. "I thought you said things were hopeful?"

Daniel's cheeks redden. "They are. That was a joke."

"Yeah?" Razim bounces a packet of potato crisps off the side of Daniel's head. "Does Katie look like she found it funny? Do I?"

"Sorry," Daniel mutters.

Moodily, Razim rips a packet of crisps open. His hand hovers, about to go into the pack, then he glances at me. "Want some?" He holds them out.

"Oh…" I shouldn't, but I still feel fragile inside. "Oh, just a few."

He tips a boy's idea of 'a few' into my hand, which

is what I'd call a lot, but what the heck.

Maybe if I was a bit plumper Shaun wouldn't be so pushy.

Someone's shaking my shoulder. I open my eyes. Joseph's leaning over me, his face barely visible in the light of a single wick.

"Joseph?"

"It's alright." His voice is very firm. "But we have to leave now."

"Now?" The silence of deep night surrounds the stable, nothing but the softest sounds coming from the livestock, and pitch blackness presses in around the single flame.

"Yes. Don't be afraid. I'll tell you all about it as soon as we're outside Bethlehem. We can't linger. Can you feed Jesus while I get the bundle packed and saddle-blanket on?"

"Of course."

He moves away, and I can see him crisscrossing the stable as he gathers our meager belongings. What's happening? Are we in danger? Despite his calmness, I sense tension.

"Joseph? Did you dream again?"

His voice comes softly to me, full of confidence in the One who has spoken to him. "Yes."

CHAPTER 5

WEDNESDAY

"Why don't you come around to my place this Saturday?" Shaun says, nuzzling my ear.

"Uh… We're not supposed to be meeting inside yet, are we?"

Shaun gives a dismissive snort. "Oh, if you're worried about that, we can hang out in the garden. There's a summerhouse we can go into. It's even got curtains."

"Uh…" My mind races. I'm just not sure I'm up for…for hanging out in Shaun's summerhouse. But if I refuse, he'll be hurt and angry. "Uh, I'd like to, but I'll have to see how I'm doing with my woodwork entry. It's, uh, not going very well."

Shaun pulls back, giving me a disgusted stare. "You're actually entering? You know I'm going to win."

I shrug. "Yeah, of course you are. But I just thought

it would be fun to try and make something cool."

Shaun rolls his eyes. "Whatever. But I'm getting on fine with mine and since you won't win, you might as well come around, right?"

"Uh…well, if I'm far enough on with it. I know it won't be very good, but I don't want to turn in something that's not actually finished."

Shaun tenses, but he speaks in a friendly tone. "Oh, did you hear about Tracy in my year? Her boyfriend— well, ex-boyfriend, very ex—put photos of her online. She's not in school today. I s'pose knowing half the guys in your class have seen *rather* a lot does make a girl cry."

My skin goes cold, like I've just taken an ice-shower. Why is he telling me that?

His arms slip around me, drawing me close. "What a scumbag," he breaths, his minty breath on my face. "I would *never* do that to you."

I try to relax as he lowers his lips to mine. *See!* Guilt twists inside me. How could I think he was actually… What sort of girlfriend am I?

All the same, when Shaun and I part I find my feet taking me back to that quiet classroom instead of to the cafeteria. The door is ajar as I approach, and I hear Daniel's voice.

"But doesn't it bother you, Raz? He's a creep!"

Razim's voice replies, "She's not my sister, Daniel. Girls throw themselves at predators all the time. What can *we* do? It's her choice…"

I stop short, heat rushing into my face. Are they talking about me? But why would they be talking about me? Why would I even think that? Of course they're not talking about me! Because that would mean they were talking about Shaun, and Shaun's not a…a creep! A…*predator*! He's super-fit, he's smart, he's good at so many things, and I'm so lucky to be his girlfriend.

Yeah, my friends treat me like I'm so important, now, when before I was just Katie the new girl, cool enough to hang out with them but nothing special. Any of them would love to be Shaun's girlfriend. If I don't sound enthusiastic enough when I speak about him, they look at me like I'm mad. A mad cockroach. Guess that's one reason I'm avoiding the cafeteria.

I end up hiding in the girls' toilet until it's time for class.

I try to carry on with the saint project when I get home, but I'm struggling to concentrate. I keep thinking about Saturday and Shaun's summerhouse. I want to talk to someone, but I cannot, cannot, cannot mention this to Mum. She doesn't even know I'm dating Shaun. And she absolutely mustn't find out about the picture. What if she did think there must be others? Worse ones?

She said just recently—finally!—that she thought I might be old enough to go out on a date once Covid is over. Nothing would change her mind faster than seeing that picture!

I open my desk drawer and dig out the framed photo of Dad I keep hidden at the bottom, where Mum won't see it. But I only stare at it for a moment before shoving it away again. Dad doesn't care anymore. Even though he claimed the only reason he didn't end it with his boss was because he was so afraid of losing his job and not being able to provide for us, he hasn't contacted me in *three years*, so he must've been lying. I've no idea how to talk to him anyway, where he is. At least none of my friends know anything more than that he and Mum are divorced. I couldn't bear it if they found out the rest.

I go back to reading the papal letter. I've got to make some progress with this. One line jumps out at me. Joseph is "the man who goes unnoticed, a daily, discreet and hidden presence—an intercessor, a support and a guide in times of trouble." My throat's gone all tight again. I need someone like that in my life so badly! Shaun just doesn't make me feel like that and my dad's turned his back on me.

"Saint Joseph," I whisper. "I wish *you* were my father. I wish you could make my father care again. Or teach my boyfriend how to be like you." My eyes fall on the pile of wooden parts that is my competition entry.

31

"Or even help me finish that!"

I can't just quote this papal letter, though, I need more. I return to Google and soon have a list of devotions. Rosary of Saint Joseph? I had no idea there was such a thing. And what's this? Novena of the Holy Cloak of Saint Joseph. I picture Saint Joseph laying his cloak over Mary as she sleeps by a roadside, I picture little Jesus hiding behind it, tugging on it in play. What an adorable idea for a prayer!

I open the novena page. Disappointingly, the prayer seems to be quite lengthy and written in old-fashioned flowery language, interspersed with lots of Glory Bes. And you're supposed to say it daily for *thirty days*. I scroll down, quickly. Yep, I'll simply mention it in my project...

But part of the final prayer catches my eye:

> From this moment on, I choose you as my father, my protector, my counselor, my patron and I beseech you to place in your custody my body, my soul, all that I am, all that I possess, my life and my death.
>
> Look upon me as one of your children; defend me from the treachery of my enemies, invisible or otherwise, assist me at all times in all my necessities;

console me in the bitterness of my life, and especially at the hour of my death.

Wow! Daniel would like the bits about death, but...this is just what I was wanting—Saint Joseph as my father! Saying this prayer will make it official! But...*thirty days*? One thought of Shaun and the summerhouse and the photo and that impossibly complicated wood-working plan makes up my mind. A new father is worth saying a few prayers for thirty days. And I'm going to do it properly, like I mean it. Because I do.

I print the prayer off, then go and sit quietly in the corner of my room. I read it out loud, and I speak slowly enough that I can take in what I'm saying, even though a lot of it is elaborate old-fashioned language that alternates between weird and embarrassing. But the final prayer makes my heart swell with a strange feeling of hope.

It's only as I say the very last part that I realise I'm committing myself to slightly more than thirty days of prayer: "Say but one word for me to the Divine Redeemer Whom you were deemed worthy to hold in your arms, and to the Blessed Virgin Mary, your most chaste spouse. Request for me those blessings which will lead me to salvation. Include me amongst those who are most dear to you and I shall set forth to prove myself worthy of your special patronage. Amen."

Prove myself worthy. How do I do that?

CHAPTER 6

THURSDAY

"So, are you on for Saturday?" Shaun asks, stretching his arms up towards the ceiling until his shirt lifts free of his trousers, flashing a glimpse of his rock-hard abs.

I've thought about this a lot. I know what I have to say. It's not unreasonable. But my heart pounds in my throat. "It's really disappointing, but I don't think I'll be able to. Making a whole competition entry on top of all my coursework—it's a bit crazy fitting it all in. Next week should be quieter." Ignoring the little voice that's asking me if I really want to go to Shaun's summer-house next weekend either, I wait breathlessly for his response.

To my surprise, he just shrugs. "You're really keen on that stupid entry, aren't you? Well, if you're going to do a thing, you might as well do it as well as you can, isn't that what they say?"

He understands? Relief floods through me, then shame. Why shouldn't he understand? Why am I always thinking the worst of him?

He lowers his face for a kiss, and for once it's easy to respond. Until, for some reason, Saint Joseph pops into my head. Would he not approve? I mean, we're just kissing, right?

Shaun senses my sudden lack of enthusiasm and draws away slightly. "Heck, now what?"

"I...I just...suddenly remembered something I'd forgotten. It was a little distracting. Sorry."

Shaun sighs. "I suppose you must have to juggle quite a lot of things. Do you have to fit in visiting your father at the weekend, as well?"

Visiting... Ice freezes my spine solid, like a frozen plant stem in the winter. No, he can't know! He just knows my parents are divorced. That's what he means...

"Uh..." My voice shakes. *Stay calm, silly, he doesn't know!* "Uh, not this weekend."

"I suppose it must be quite a fiasco. Do they search you, when you enter the prison?"

A wave of coldness washes over me and buzzing fills my ears. He knows! How does he know? Well, how did *I* find out? But why was he Googling my father?

Should I deny it all? That would be lying, and what's the point? It's true.

36

"I…I don't see him very much." Understatement.

"Right. I s'pose it is a bit embarrassing. I'm kinda hurt you didn't tell your boyfriend, though."

"Of course I was going to," I whisper. "But—"

"I suppose you haven't told your friends, either? If my dad was in prison I wouldn't want all my friends to know. It would be a shame if they found out. Of course, *boyfriends* keep their mouths shut about such things."

Why did he emphasize that word? My ears are still buzzing and nausea churns my stomach. Is he threatening to tell my friends? Why am I jumping to that conclusion? He hasn't said that! He just said the opposite.

Trying to smile at him, I speak warmly. "I know I can trust *you*, Shaun. No question."

He pulls me in for another kiss. When he releases me, he murmurs, "So I'll see you on Saturday, then."

And walks away.

I run all the way to the loos, I'm so afraid I'm going to throw up. But after hanging over the toilet for a while, gasping and sobbing and clutching my long blonde hair out of the way, the feeling eases.

"What do I do?" I whisper. "Saint Joseph, you're supposed to be sorting this out and it's just got a million times worse! What do I *do?*"

+

Saint Joseph doesn't speak in my head, but eventually I find myself putting my mask back on to hide as much of my face as possible and all but running through the corridors to my year group classroom. I slam through the door, my eyes raking the room. Daniel's there. A lunch box but no Razim. Gone to the vending machine? Thank God!

I shut the door tight and slump into a chair, my hands clenched on the desktop. They're shaking, and I can't stop them.

"Katie, are you okay?"

I pull my mask off, even though it lets him see my blotchy red face, and put my hands over my eyes.

"I think… I think…" I'm starting to cry again as, unstoppably, I blurt it out, "I think Shaun's trying to blackmail me…but I'm not sure…and…and…"

"It's okay," says Daniel, staring at me with big calm grey eyes. "Just…start at the beginning. Or…have a cry first, if you need to. Sometimes you just need to."

He makes it sound like 'having a cry' is a natural thing that everyone does, even sixteen-year-old boys, and his understanding actually helps me to calm down enough to talk properly. It all spills out. The photo and everything.

"…And if I don't go to Shaun's summerhouse on Saturday, he's going to tell everyone my dad's in prison. Tell everyone that after Dad's boss told my

38

mum what was going on because Dad wouldn't, Dad stole a ton of money from his boss's company in revenge and got caught and sent to prison. All the sordid details are on the internet. No wonder Mum and I moved twice since then! And if my mum sees that photo! My life *literally* will not be worth living at home or at school!"

"Well" — for a moment there's an edge to Daniel's voice — "if life-swapping were a thing, I'd accept yours happily enough."

Heck! My cheeks burn as I review what I just said. And yet...

Daniel's glancing down at his lunchbox, his own pale cheeks reddening. "I'm sorry," he says quickly, "that wasn't helpful. It's absolutely right that you're upset and worried about this. *I'm* upset and worried about this. I know someone who'll know what to do, though. Is it okay if I ask them? I won't say who you are."

"You really know someone you think can help?"

"With advice, definitely."

"Then yes!" Relief rushes through me. I don't have a clue what to do and, from Daniel's expression as he listened, he doesn't either. But he knows someone... Thanks, Saint Joseph!

"I'll tell you what he says tomorrow. Maybe try to avoid Shaun for now?"

39

Those few words and all my certainty and relief shatter. Shame rushes back. "But...I don't actually *know*...he might not be doing *anything*! I made it all sound so bad, but he hasn't said *anything* straight out. I might just be a horrible person who's taken everything the wrong way and..."

Daniel holds up a hand, begging me to stop. "Katie, put your hand on your heart"—he presses a hand to his chest in demonstration—"and tell me, *from your heart,* what you think Shaun is doing. Not with your head, not rationalizing or trying to explain it away because you don't want it to be true. From your heart, do you feel Shaun is pressurizing you?"

I drop my eyes to my hands. They'd almost stopped shaking, but now they're trembling again.

Eventually, I whisper, "Yes."

Even though it feels like I'm crushing a beautiful dream to dust with my tongue.

I keep my hands in my lap as I wait for Joseph to speak, fighting to keep them still. Yesterday, he listened, his face resolute, only the wideness of his eyes betraying the depths of his hurt. Every now and then, they flicked to my belly, to the curve that betrays my condition. My cousin Elizabeth wanted me to stay with her until I'd had the baby. She promised to pass the child discreetly to a wealthy childless couple. I could have come home and married Joseph, all as planned.

But I knew I couldn't do that. Nothing about what God told me suggested I was supposed to give the child He entrusted to me away, or to deceive Joseph. *God will take care of me and the child. Somehow.*

When I'd finished the tale, I risked another glance at Joseph's face. He hadn't spoken, as I told him all. I waited for his anger. *I am his betrothed wife, and as far as he can know, I have disgraced him. Betrayed him.* But after a long silence, Joseph just said he would speak to me today. That he needed to think and pray.

Now he will tell me what he has decided. He can have me stoned in the street. Or he can divorce me quietly. What else can he do?

But which will he choose? No need to worry about the future if he chooses the full measure of the Law. But if he spares me? How will I raise my special baby?

No, I must be calm and not worry. God knows I cannot raise this baby by myself.

"Mary," Joseph says at last, his voice almost steady, "you know I have a very high opinion of you. It was difficult for me to believe you would lie, but yesterday there seemed to be no reasonable explanation. I had decided to divorce you quietly, but something happened last night that changed my mind."

Despite my certainty that God is in command, coldness washes through me. He's changed his mind? I'm to be stoned?

41

"While I slept, an angel of the Lord spoke to me. Everything you told me was confirmed, every detail. The Lord orders me to take you as my wife and care for the child as my own."

His brown eyes meet mine, warm, firm, and touched with awe. "I do not know why he has chosen me, of all men. But I will do exactly as He commands. If by my life or my death I can protect you and the baby, I will. You have my word."

CHAPTER 7

FRIDAY

Avoiding the corridor where I normally meet Shaun, I creep to our year group classroom at lunchtime, desperate to know if Daniel has found out anything useful. I felt so much better after talking to him yesterday I got a surprising amount of work done in the evening.

I also read about a charming Saint Joseph 'devotion' where you place a list of prayers under a statue of Saint Joseph sleeping—because he got most of his instructions from God in dreams, I suppose. Kinda letting Saint Joseph sleep on your problems. Since I don't have a real statue, I printed off a picture of one and wrote a list to slip underneath:

Shaun
Dad

It felt good to do something physical, even if it's just symbolic.

Then I worked on the competition entry for several hours. I've finished making all the parts and I've painted them and they're really looking good. But when I turn to the plans and try to put it together... helplessness and despair enfold me. Have I wasted all this effort? Still, last night, working on it was better than sitting around alternating between worry about Shaun and feeling filthy-wretched.

Right now, I've reached the classroom. Daniel's already here, but Razim's lunchbox isn't in sight today, nor is he. Has Daniel asked him to stay away? I'm really grateful, though I hope he doesn't mind too much. He showed up yesterday and didn't say a word about my red eyes.

"Hi, Daniel." I sit far enough away and slip my mask off.

Daniel smiles. "Hi, Katie. Well, Father Thomas had some good advice."

"You asked a priest?" I blurt.

He looks surprised "Why not? People go to him with things like this all the time."

I don't know why I'm so surprised. I suppose I've never seen a priest as someone you just casually go to and ask stuff. They're, like, important and busy and unapproachable, in my mind. My mum avoids them like the plague, since divorcing Dad. I know a lot of people would think she was right to do it, but it never felt right, to me, despite what Dad had done. Dad begged her not to. On his knees. I saw. I don't know what a priest would say about it—though I'm starting to want to.

Father Thomas—that's the priest I saw at Christmas, I think. Tall, young, very dark skin, big smile and lots of enthusiasm. I liked him.

I focus on Daniel. "Okay, what did he suggest?"

"Well, with regard to the photo, he said the best thing you can do is tell your mum about it yourself."

"What?"

"Well, that's what I thought initially, but he made some good points. He said if you tell her, you preempt anything Shaun can do. She'll respect that you told her, she'll be on your side, and she'll be a hundred times more likely to believe that it was just one photo. You cut the ground from under Shaun; he's got nothing left to pressurize you with."

"Uh, except my father!"

"Yeah, and his advice there is the same: Tell your friends. It's not good keeping something that big back, always watching what you say, always afraid they'll find out anyway. Much better to be upfront about it."

"But…" Horror fills me at the thought of my friends knowing. "But…what if they don't want to hang out with me anymore?"

Daniel frowns. "Then they're not your friends."

He says it so simply, but I feel like he's punched me in the gut. The only good thing about moving yet again was that when I started this school, I found myself in the coolest group. Not really at the very centre until I got together with Shaun. But still, I was *in*. The position I'd dreamed of for so long. But sometimes I miss my original school, the one I was at before Dad… Even though I was just boring Katie everyone had known from junior school. Everything with my new friends just seems less…genuine. Sometimes I've caught myself wondering how deep our friendships actually go.

Daniel's right. If I can't even tell them about my dad, are they really my friends at all?

I frown at the desktop, my mind churning. I feel trapped between Shaun and everything that I'm supposed to want, and…what's my other choice? Freaky Daniel and his loyal friend? Elena told me Razim used to be quite an undersized kid, always getting thrashed by his brother. Now he's shot up and his shoulders have broadened out and he's got really good-looking. He could totally be in the cool set, she said, if he ditched Daniel. His current hairless condition makes it clear how likely that is.

46

Can I really imagine throwing in with Daniel and Razim? The weirdoes? I wince. But…but I don't feel like I need to hide and keep up appearances near them. I can't believe all the stuff I've told Daniel, but he seems like such a safe pair of ears. I can just…be myself. Would it really be so bad if I told my friends about my dad? But not wanting to hang out any more is one thing, but what if they're mean about it? What if the entire school gets to hear about it? What if *everyone's* mean?

I eye Daniel. 'The Jesus-freak with cancer,' that's what Shaun called him. Daniel knows what it's like to be a target but he doesn't seem bothered. Because of his faith, I suppose. But I don't have faith like that. I'm starting to wish I did, but I don't…

Daniel can tell I'm even less keen on this suggestion than the last one, because he says, "Think about it, someone will probably find out eventually, even if Shaun doesn't tell them. If you preempt him, you can keep any real friends you've made and take away the power he has over you at the same time."

Take away the power… I've been letting him *kiss* me because I'm too scared to pull away. And that makes me feel…I don't even want to think about how that makes me feel. Daniel's right. I've got to get free of him.

"As for the photo…"

"What?" Didn't we cover that already? "Oh, the internet threat?"

"Yes. That's actually the biggest danger, Father Thomas says. Once it's online, it's incredibly hard to eradicate it, and very often your name will be attached to it. Every time anyone searches for you in future, for a job or anything, it will pop up."

For a *job?* Cold prickles erupt all over my skin. Every time I apply for a job my prospective boss will see me in just my towel, trying to look all sexy? Of course they will. I've been so busy worrying about my *mum...* How could I be so stupid? Heat rushes into my cheeks. Have I just wrecked my future with one dumb photo, trying to please a...a predator-creep?

If he *is*. If I'm not wrong...

Oh shut up! I tell myself, then say, "Please tell me there's something I can do?"

"This is where it will really help if you tell your mum. Because Father Thomas says the best way to stop it getting online in the first place is to get a really scary letter from a lawyer making your copyright of the photograph crystal-clear and requiring Shaun to delete any copies that he has under pain of legal action. Also containing a detailed run-down of the law if he puts it online. Two years in prison, apparently, if convicted."

Two *years?* Shaun will never risk that! Relief fills me—until I remember...

"But my mum will totally freak out!" Is this really a good idea? How can I tell her? Maybe I should just keep quiet and hope Shaun doesn't do it...

Daniel leans forward, his eyes intent. "Katie, you've gotta tell you mum, seriously. I've never seen Father Thomas so worried. He told me some stuff...this sort of thing gets really bad, Katie."

He looks worried, too.

"What did he tell you?"

Daniel hesitates. "Well...it's not nice...okay, fine, he said just this autumn there was a girl in a nearby school who kept sending—you know, call it virtual gifts—to her boyfriend on her phone, all through the Lockdown. And then in December she found out he'd been two-timing her with some girl whose parents didn't believe in Covid and had been letting him hang out at their house."

"That's horrible."

"Yeah, anyway, she dumped him, as he totally deserved. But the twisted twerp was offended—offended, can you believe?—and put all the photos online with her name attached. They spread like mad and it was clear she couldn't stop it and she obviously didn't know what to do. She never told her parents a thing. The first they found out about it was when she—" Daniel breaks off, his eyes wide and distressed. "Well...Father Thomas said he had to conduct the funeral and try to comfort her parents."

I suck in a breath, feeling like he's just punched me in the stomach even harder.

"And," Daniel's leaning forward again. "Father Thomas says that's not a one-off. He's been through it all before. He says these filthy gifts destroy people's futures, they destroy people's lives—especially girls— they cause so much harm. He said you should never, ever send them to anyone you're in any relationship with short of marriage. Actually, he said they're not great in marriage either but for totally different reasons...ah, never mind that." Daniel flaps his hand. "But Katie, do you see why you need to put a stop to it *right now*? *Please*, tell your mum."

I stare into his anxious face. I would never... Surely I would never... But what if I hadn't even told Daniel? What if I was trying to deal with it all by myself? That terrible feeling of oppression the other night...the wretchedness I've been feeling, submitting to Shaun's kisses out of fear...feeling so sure I couldn't tell my mum or friends...is it possible to spiral that far down into despair?

I s'pose it is, because it happens...

"Please?" Daniel isn't letting it go. "Surely you realize your mum would a hundred times rather hear about it now from you, than..."

"Okay, okay!"

"Promise?"

"Yes, I promise. I'll tell her as soon as I get home."

Daniel lets out a relieved breath and sits back in his chair, absentmindedly pulling some lettuce from a piece of sandwich and nibbling it.

I've *promised*. I'm committed. To *telling my mum*. I groan and rest my head on the desk for a moment—then realize that mostly I just feel a deep sense of relief. There *is* a way out of this that doesn't involve going into summerhouses with Shaun as often as he likes until he gets bored of me. Or...worse—Daniel's story still fills my mind, making goose bumps crawl up my back—and Daniel's found it for me.

I sit up again. "Thank you," I tell him.

He waves this aside. "How's your Saint Joseph project going?"

"A lot better than my woodwork project," I say glumly.

"For the competition? What are you making?"

"Well..." I can feel myself reddening. "I saw these—they're called automata—at a museum in the summer—no, the previous summer, pre-Covid—and I thought they were really fun. You wind a handle and they move like puppets, do you know the things I mean?"

Daniel nods, so I continue, "Well, when I heard about the competition, I googled online and there were plans for all the different moving parts for making them. I put the right plans together to make a man sawing logs—a carpenter. And the puppet parts have come out really nicely. But, honestly? I don't know that I can get it together and working. Just looking at the plans gives me a headache."

To my surprise, Daniel simply smiles. "Well, I was about to tell you about a tradition called Saint Joseph's table…"

The door opens a crack and Razim looks in. When Daniel beckons, he settles into his usual seat without any comment on why he wasn't here sooner, and hands Daniel a chocolate bar before offering me one. Since I'm celebrating stage one of getting free of Shaun—having a plan—I accept it with a smile and a mouthed "thank you."

"Especially in Italy," Daniel is saying, "they have this big feast in honor of Saint Joseph, usually on the nineteenth of March, his feast day. I've been reading about Saint Joseph because it's his year, and I wanted us to have one. But I spent most of March puking so Mum said we could do it once I'd finished chemo. Tomorrow, in fact. Razim's coming, and my mum and dad and my little sister. I was hoping to have a few of the youth group round but my mum started freaking out about too many germs around me, even though we'll be in the garden. But she did say you can come. If you'd like to.

And it's perfect because if you bring your automaton and Razim brings his tools, I'm sure he can help you get it going."

"Huh?" Razim looks up warily from his phone. "What's that I've just been volunteered for?"

CHAPTER 8

SATURDAY

"I told my mum," I say quietly to Daniel the following day, as he leads me through his house to the garden.

I did it as soon as I got home from school, just as planned, so I couldn't bottle out of it. Because it was Friday and there wasn't long before the end of office hours, she left me sitting on the sofa while she went and called her lawyer right away. Mum doesn't mess around about things like that. Only then did she come back to finish our 'talk.'

"How did it go?"

"She was disappointed." My stomach squirms in memory. "And...she almost wasn't going to let me come today. But in the end she said she was also really impressed by the maturity I'd shown by coming to her about it. She's keeping half my allowance back until the lawyer's fees are paid, though—and you would not believe what that single letter is going to cost!—but other than that she says I'm clearly grown-up enough to have learned my lesson without her punishing me like a child."

Daniel gives me a pleased smile, then we're emerging into his back garden. A little girl of about six or seven rushes over and jumps up and down in front of me, clapping her hands, the Covid-era equivalent of an excited hug.

"Hello, Katie!" she squeals.

I realize I don't know her name, but Daniel introduces her as Clare, then finds me somewhere to put the large plastic storage box I'm clutching, which contains my half-constructed automaton. Razim lifts the lid a little, trying to peep inside, but Daniel's mum swoops and presses it down firmly. "No, no, no, Engineer-Brain, food first. Then you can use the garden table."

"Wow!" I say, looking at the table. A Saint Joseph statue stands in the centre, with candles and flowers around it, and a feast winds its way around as though going up a hill to the statue. It looks mostly vegetarian, "because of its historical roots during Lent," Daniel informs us, before launching into an enthusiastic grace. Razim smiles politely instead of saying Amen, but with a name like Razim Sadiq I wouldn't expect anything else.

Each dish has a symbolic meaning and it's clear Daniel wants to explain each one in more detail than most people really want to hear, but his parents—and even Razim—just listen patiently, as though simply having Daniel standing there chattering cheerfully at them is a pleasure to be savored. Maybe it is.

Trying to ignore the sudden coldness in my belly that thought causes, I listen carefully, hoping to glean something for my project, but most of the symbolism isn't specifically about Saint Joseph, even though the feast's in his honor. Daniel also explains that he couldn't find out what all the food should be and couldn't get hold of everything he could find out about, so he's invented some of the symbolism himself.

"The feast started in Sicily in the fifteenth century," Daniel tells me, once we've devoured the first course and I ask why Saint Joseph has this 'Saint Joseph's Table' thing in the first place. "They had a terrible famine caused by a lack of rain, and they prayed like mad to Saint Joseph to intercede for them, and it rained. So, once they gathered their harvest, they had a big feast in thanksgiving. And it spread from there."

"Well, no complaints that it's spread to your garden," says Razim, biting into a fat slice of apple pie (the defeat of original sin).

"Saint Joseph doesn't have a lot of miracles associated with him, though, does he?" I say, tearing a piece off my triquetra-shaped pretzel (the Holy Trinity). "Not like Mary or some saints."

"True," says Daniel, popping a creamy mini chocolate profiterole (the pearl without price) into his mouth. "He's a very humble, quiet saint, staying in the background, just like in the Bible narratives. He never says one word, you know? Yet God gives far more instructions to him than to Mary. Makes sense he's the Guardian of the Church."

"I'm guessing that's an important position?" Razim sounds a little bored, but he seems unfazed by the persistent religious conversation. I suppose he must be used to it.

"Definitely," says Daniel. "But he does have a few miracles to his name. I mean, big famous ones. There must be millions of small, personal ones. Teresa of Avila chose him as her personal intercessor and was never refused anything. Of course, she was a saint so she probably only asked for really holy things."

I remember how my sense of oppression went away the other night. Was that a small, personal miracle or was it too minor to count? All in a night's work for the Terror of Demons?

"There's the miraculous spring in France, for example," Daniel continues. "A tired shepherd called Gaspard was desperately thirsty when Saint Joseph appeared and ordered him to lift a massive boulder. He shouldn't have been able to pick it up, but he did, and a spring bubbled up from beneath it."

Razim is eyeing my box again.

"There have been quite a few apparitions, too," says Daniel, then breaks off to yawn. "But I can't remember all the details."

His mum and dad start clearing things from the table, with the help cum hindrance of little Clare. I try to help too, but they wave me away, smiling. I eye Daniel's dad with a mix of longing and envy. Will I ever have a physical dad again? A spiritual dad is certainly nicer than nothing at all, but... Oh, never mind.

Once I've finished setting out the pieces of my would-be automaton on the freshly-wiped table, I turn to find that Daniel's now drawn his legs into his egg-shaped hanging seat and gone to sleep, curled up like a dormouse, and Razim's tucking a blanket over him.

"Is he okay?"

"Oh, yeah. He still nods off now and then. Hasn't got his energy back yet. I just make sure I have a phone or a project or a book to hand."

"He seemed to have a bunch of friends at the beginning of the year." I can't but notice that it's just Razim here at this thing. And me.

Razim scowls. "Yeah, well, we thought he did. They just drifted off after he got ill."

I twist my hands together. "Maybe...maybe they

just didn't know what to say?"

Razim shakes his head angrily. "I didn't know what to say. I still don't. Especially when he goes all morbid. No reason to abandon a friend. It's low."

Frantic to change the subject, I turn back to the table and grab the print-out of the inscrutable plans. "So, uh, I've got all the puppet bits made. And I think I have all the right rods and cogs and things. But I'm struggling with putting it together."

Razim takes the plans and seems to understand them in one glance. "Okay, I see, so the carpenter's right arm moves all the time, sawing the logs. And the logs go around on the belt, but they only move forward every fourth turn of the handle, so it looks like they're being chopped and falling into the basket. And then the little kid tugs on the carpenter's robe every six turns."

"Yeah." I made the child just this morning, as an extra. The paint was barely dry when it was time to box it up. "I didn't want the child tugging all the time because it would look like the carpenter was ignoring the child, and he wouldn't do that."

"Is it Jesus and Joseph?"

"Uh…" My face heats up. I'm not used to being all openly religious, like Daniel is, but that is why I added the little boy. "Well, I consider it, um, what's the artistic phrase, open to interpretation. But to me, uh, yeah, it's Jesus and Joseph."

"It's really neat."

"Well, in theory. I can't get it together."

"Oh, it's pretty straight forward. Especially with the plans. Let's see…" Razim begins muttering to himself as he opens a toolbox and picks up different parts and begins to slot them into the housing box for the mechanism, which I'm pleased to say I *have* managed to get together.

I hover for a while, feeling like I should be helping, but Razim is soon so engrossed I feel like I'm only distracting him. I go and sit on a garden bench a little way from Daniel and just watch. It's no hardship. Even with that short buzz of stubble on his head, Razim's handsome. His hands move, strong and confident, as they assemble the parts.

Does Razim even count as my friend, after the limited contact we've had? Yet there he is, working on my automaton when my supposedly wonderful boyfriend never even asked what I was making. It smarts to realize how blind I've been about Shaun. How much his good looks and my friends' adulation have fogged my mind.

Eventually Daniel wakes up, yawning and stretching before putting his legs out of the hanging chair and sitting up properly. "I'm sorry," he says to me, "I can be rather boring, these days."

"It's fine," I say quickly. "I'm just sitting here

feeling bad that Razim is doing all the work."

Daniel glances at his friend and grins. "Ah, he's having a great time, don't worry. He loves taking things apart and putting them together."

"I can hear you, man," says Razim, bent over with his nose inches from the automaton as he makes some fiddly adjustment.

"Am I telling lies about you?"

"Nope." Razim straightens and flashes us a grin. "Well, I think it's done. Though"—he eyes the automaton but then, for some reason, shoots a look at Daniel—"I do have this *really* cool idea..."

I look out of the window into the courtyard as I stir the stew, watching Jesus working hard on a tiny child-sized table while Joseph works on a full-sized one. He's such a hard-working little boy and He always wants to do what His abba is doing. He helps me a lot with household chores, of course, the way He should at His age, but He's already learning carpentry from Joseph.

A wail pierces straight to my heart and my eyes rise from the stew, fixing on Jesus again. I've almost dropped the spoon to rush outside before I check myself. Joseph is right there...

Yes, Joseph is already sweeping Jesus up in his arms. A bruised finger is kissed, Jesus is tossed in the air and caught a few times, already He's giggling, happy again. Joseph sets Him back on the paving slabs, takes His tiny hand in his, picks up the little hammer and starts showing Him a safer way to hit the nails.

"But sometimes I feel so scared of nails," comes Jesus's little voice, quivering again.

Joseph scoops Jesus onto his lap. "There's no need to be scared of nails," he assures Him. "Or hammers. Or anything at all. Remember, God is the God of the whole universe, and so long as we do what is pleasing to Him, we should fear nothing. God will ensure all is as it should be."

Silence for a moment. Then Jesus pipes up happily, reciting, "The Lord is on my side; I will not fear. What can man do to me?"

I don't need to see Joseph's face to see that he's beaming with pride. He loves it when Jesus remembers a scripture verse he's taught Him.

"Exactly right."

"Yes, I shouldn't be afraid of anything. Not even the *new billy-goat."*

Joseph back-tracks hastily. "Well, a little caution with that crazy goat would be a good idea. If You get Yourself butted from here to Jerusalem Your amma will not be happy."

"Maybe I'll tame the billy!"

"Maybe You will," laughs Joseph. "But first, let's finish these tables."

CHAPTER 9

SUNDAY

I didn't look at my phone yesterday evening, but when I reluctantly take a peep on Sunday morning I find a string of messages from Shaun.

Are you coming over?

When are you getting here?

Are you on the way?

Katie, where are you?

Are you ignoring me?

Guilt squeezes my chest. He's still my boyfriend, right? Officially? I probably should've told him I wasn't coming. But then I read on.

How's your father?

How about another picture?

Why are you ignoring me?

I toss my phone on my bed, furious. He's *still* trying to... *Uh, forget him, Katie!*

It was late in the afternoon before I left Daniel's house, by the time Razim finished tinkering with the automaton and we all chatted loads and Daniel's mum kept bringing us out plates of leftovers and Clare wanted to sing us a song. When will Shaun get the letter? Mum said I should avoid him until he gets it, but maybe I ought to break up with him first?

Break up with him? My heart thumps in my chest, like it's doing a double back-flip. Am I really going to break up with—

Ugh! No! He's *not* a wonderful boyfriend. How can I still be thinking like this?

I throw myself on the bed beside my phone. The automaton is finished—my goodness, is it finished! Razim's idea turned out *so* well. I've got to complete my saint project, then Daniel and Razim will be in a local park this afternoon flying a hovercraft or something—a little one, I presume—and they invited me to join them.

The sun's out and it's a lovely day, so I think I will.

I've got some texts from my friends too, inviting me to do stuff—all outdoors, of course—but I don't want to have to pretend things are okay with Shaun or, even worse, tell them I mean to break up with him until I've done it. So I'll just hang out quietly with Daniel and Razim today.

I turn my laptop on and work for a while, pulling all my Saint Joseph information together. I need a strong conclusion, though...

Am I really going to break up with Shaun? Really?

Pushing the stupid voice aside, I open the papal letter again. I've read most of it, but not to the end. Maybe there's something good... What's this?

Joseph is traditionally called a "most chaste" father. That title is not simply a sign of affection, but the summation of an attitude that is the opposite of possessiveness. Chastity is freedom from possessiveness in every sphere of one's life. Only when love is chaste, is it truly love. A possessive love ultimately becomes dangerous: it imprisons, constricts and makes for misery.

My heart pounding, I read the words again.

Possessive love...dangerous...imprisons...misery... It could be a description of my brief relationship with Shaun!

I read on:

God himself loved humanity with a chaste love; he left us free even to go astray and set ourselves against him. The logic of love is always the logic of freedom, and Joseph knew how to love with extraordinary freedom. He never made himself the centre of things. He did not think of himself, but focused instead on the lives of Mary and Jesus.

He didn't think of himself...

My eyes find one more line: "Our world today needs fathers. It has no use for tyrants who would domineer others as a means of compensating for their own needs."

Breathing as though I've been running, I push away from the desk and grab my phone from the bed. I've typed a short message when I stop, my finger hovering over 'send.' With a sigh, I delete it. No. I *am* definitely, one hundred percent dumping Shaun. But not by text. Maybe he doesn't deserve anything more, but I'm not that low. I'll tell him face-to-face.

I return to my project and work the quote in. One more search on Google for Saint Joseph and 'most chaste father' brings up something new. 'The Cord of Saint Joseph.' I click on it and read more. You can wear a white cord with seven knots around your waist as a physical way to ask Saint Joseph's help, especially with chastity, and as a reminder to yourself as well. Apparently it's like the Angelic Warfare Confraternity—whatever that is—but easier to do because you don't have to be officially enrolled or make a lifelong commitment.

A physical symbol...like a pledge. *Prove myself worthy.* The words come back into my head. Kissing boys I've no intention of marrying isn't 'proving myself worthy,' is it? I tried to pretend to myself I didn't know why Saint Joseph popped into my head like that the other day, but I do really.

Not even kissing? *Are you serious?* moans a voice in my head. I ignore it, because the cord has set my blood racing with a weird, fierce longing and I'm too busy searching for places to buy one.

Sold out. Everywhere. Because it's the Year of Saint Joseph? But...wait, it says you can just make one.

A few minutes later I've found a simple piece of white wool and made seven knots at one end—representing the seven joys and sorrows in Saint Joseph's life—and I'm holding it up, staring at it. If I tie

67

this around my waist and recite those prayers I'm turning my back on everything I thought I wanted, everything I've tried to embrace since Mum and Dad divorced. My friends will think I've gone stark religious crazy, like Daniel, if they find out. But then, if they care, are they my friends?

Something about that simple cord sings of...of freedom.

If I put this on, I'm taking responsibility—I'm taking control—I'll never again kiss someone because I feel like I *should* want to, I'll kiss someone only when and if I want to, when it's right, when it won't make me unworthy of my spiritual father.

I'll wait for a chaste man, who wants to *give himself* to me, not *possess me.*

Heck, yeah!

I raise my top a little and tie the cord carefully around my waist. And I recite the prayers. I'm supposed to get the cord blessed sometime, as well, but that will have to wait. I say my Saint Joseph's Cloak novena prayers too, the way I've been doing every day.

Then I've just time to finish my project before lunch.

CHAPTER 10

SUNDAY

The hovercraft *is* small, less than two feet long and radio-controlled, but it really is a hovercraft, levitating over the ground. Razim turns it upside down and explains how it works, nursing it like a proud father, but all I really understand is that the fan holds it up with blown air.

He lets me take it for a spin, though, and there's a lot of good-humored laughter from the two boys as I get to grips with the controls. Daniel takes a turn too, but once Razim and I have driven it up and down the bank and out onto the lake and back to our heart's content we find Daniel's lain down on the grass and gone to sleep.

Fore-sighted Razim produces a blanket from his rucksack which he settles over Daniel, then he asks me to stay there while he fetches ice-creams from the park kiosk. I'm relaxing, enjoying the spring sunshine, when

I notice a group of familiar faces from school not that far away. A couple of my friends—Elena and Cara—are tagging along with four older kids…and one of them is Shaun.

Oh heck. Here I am, sitting with *Daniel*…my cheeks go hot. Then I'm ashamed of being so embarrassed. I mean, I've had more fun with Daniel and Razim in the last two days than I've had since I joined this school. And if I want to break up with Shaun before he gets the letter, now would be a good time. Probably the only time.

Daniel's sleeping quietly, so I get up and head over to the group. My heart's pounding like mad. If I didn't know that letter was on the way…if this wasn't going to be ten times more awkward afterwards…nothing would make me do this, otherwise, in front of all these older kids. And Elena and Cara. *Saint Joseph, help!*

"Shaun? Could I have a word?"

Shaun turns and looks me up and down. "Well, look who it is. I hope you've got a good reason for standing me up like that."

I realize I'm gripping two handfuls of my jacket hem and try to let go. "*I* never said I was coming, Shaun. *I* said I was too busy. Could I have a word with you for a moment?"

With an ill grace he follows me a little way from the rest of the group, who stare after us, clearly wagging their ears. "Where were you?" he demands, once we stand under the shade of a nearby tree that gives a slight illusion of privacy.

"That's really none of your business."

"Really? Corey saw you coming out of loser Daniel's house yesterday evening. And I do believe that's loser Daniel all limp on the grass right now." Shaun jerks his head towards Daniel, then steps towards me, his whole body tense. "Are you two-timing me with that sickly Jesus-freak?"

He's really making me mad, now. "No, I'm not! Daniel is not my boyfriend. But what I want to tell you is—you're not my boyfriend anymore either. I'm breaking up with you."

He gapes at me. "You're *what?*"

"I'm breaking up with you."

"You—" Face darkening with rage, he moves so fast he's gripping my arms and pressing me back against the tree before I can react.

"*Get off—*"

"*You're* breaking up with *me*? How dare you! Do you know how many girls would love to—"

"Get off me!"

"I will tell *everyone*—"

"Tell them what you like!" My heart's hammering, my eyes watering with pain from his tight grip on my arms. *Saint Joseph, help!* "*I'm* going to tell them if you

71

don't! Now, let me go!"

"In your dreams."

"Shaun," says a calm voice. "I'm filming you. Let go of her or I'll send the video to the police. I think you need to check the definition of assault."

Shaun releases me, spinning around. Daniel's standing there, a phone in his bony hand, pointed our way. I stumble over to him, rubbing my arms, trying not to shake, but I can't help it. My body won't stop.

Shaun's trembling too as he glares at Daniel, but with rage. But after a moment he turns and starts to walk away. Daniel lowers the phone at last—and Shaun spins around and charges.

"Look out!" Too late. Daniel tosses me the phone a second before Shaun knocks him flying.

I clutch it—should I run? What about Daniel? But Shaun's following the phone, coming at me. Before he can reach me, another shape hurtles into him, carrying him right back into the trunk of the tree with a solid thud. Ow. That must've hurt. Like I care.

It's Razim, a head shorter than Shaun but looking so ferocious I'm not surprised Shaun hesitates. Or maybe he's just recovering from being slammed into the tree. Razim plants himself in front of Daniel and me like Shaun's going to have to go through him. Snapping out of my shock, I swipe at Daniel's phone hastily, but it's locked itself. I shove it in my pocket and drag mine out, tapping frantically…*quick, quick*…Razim may be furious as heck, but he really is a lot smaller than Shaun…

Fortunately it hasn't gone beyond a savage staring match when I get my camera rolling.

"Shaun, now *I'm* filming you."

This time, Shaun leaves. Or rather, storms away. I notice the group he was with giving him shocked looks, but I'm too busy crouching beside Daniel.

Daniel looks giddy, but he's pushing himself into a sitting position, all grass-stained elbows and thin arms.

"What the heck are you two doing, taking on a great big gorilla like that on your own?" demands Razim, crouching beside us now he's satisfied Shaun's really gone.

"Well, he was manhandling Katie," pants Daniel. "I figured he'd stop if he knew he was being filmed, but the guy really is a psycho. I think he was trying to steal my phone."

"Probably just going to delete the video and throw it back in your face," says Razim. "Are you definitely all right?"

Daniel pulls up a trouser leg, inspecting his shin. "Yeah, I think so. I might not even have bruises if the chemo's done its job as well as they think it has."

My insides have gone all quivery and I'm terribly afraid I'm about to cry. "I'm really sorry…"

"What are *you* apologizing for?" says Razim. "The

only person I saw doing anything he shouldn't was Shaun."

His dismissiveness wipes away the guilt that was building and, drawing deep breathes, I manage to get hold of myself while he stalks off to retrieve the blanket along with the three individually wrapped ice-creams he dropped when he saw Shaun attack Daniel. While he's gone, Shaun's group comes over to ask if Daniel is okay. They might never choose to hang out with him, but clearly they don't think anyone should be knocking him around, either. Elena even asks me if I'm okay.

"He was very rough with you," she says uneasily.

"Yeah." I take a deep breath. This may be my one chance to tell it before Shaun. I speak clearly and audibly. "He was threatening to tell everyone about my dad being in prison if I didn't, you know, *do things* with him. And I didn't think that was how a boyfriend should behave so I dumped him. That's why the loser got so angry."

Elena stares at me. I can practically see her balancing what I'm saying against her image of Shaun as such a cool, desirable guy, against how she just saw him behave with her own eyes.

"That's blackmail," she says slowly. Then, "Your dad's in prison?"

"Yeah. I'm sorry I didn't mention it. It's hard to know how to bring it up."

Elena chews her lip and stares after Shaun. Finally, she sighs regretfully. "What a loser."

Cara looks like she's ready to defend Shaun, but the kids from Shaun's year are shaking their heads as they talk among themselves. Satisfied Daniel is okay, they move away.

"Tell me about it some time," says Elena.

"Yeah, sure."

She follows the others, and Cara starts arguing with her as soon as they're out of earshot. I don't know if Elena and I will be hanging out so much in future, but at least it doesn't seem like she's going to be nasty—and that means a lot.

CHAPTER 11

MONDAY

Joseph hasn't spoken for hours now, or really focused on anything, but occasionally his lips curve into a smile as Jesus or I stroke his hair tenderly out of his eyes or moisten his lips with a damp cloth. Although my heart is breaking from the knowledge that soon he will no longer be with us, I talk to him, softly and cheerfully, reciting the psalms or reminiscing on Jesus's childhood escapades. When I grow hoarse, Jesus takes over.

Joseph has remained calm throughout these last days, except for one strange, disturbing burst of agitation and terror. Jesus said it was just something physical going on in his body and that we should simply soothe him until it passed off. As it did. Now he's silent, except for those gentle smiles, and I know the moment I dread isn't far off. But the Lord is in charge.

Joseph's trust in God has never wavered. His last words

were, "Blessed be the Lord, the God of Israel..."
He was looking at Jesus when he said them.

I wake with a start. I've had a lot of dreams about Joseph and Mary—and Jesus—since starting my project, and I've enjoyed most of them. But that one...that was so sad. Joseph dying. But so peacefully, with Jesus and Mary beside him. I suppose it wouldn't be so scary if you had Jesus and Mary with you. That must be what it meant by 'happy death.' As happy *as possible.*

It reminds me of a prayer I found while doing my research:

Jesus, Mary and Joseph, I give you my heart and
my soul.
Jesus, Mary and Joseph, assist me in my last agony.
Jesus, Mary and Joseph, may I breathe forth my
soul in peace with you.
Holy Family: Grant Me Peace. *Amen.*

I thought of writing it out for Daniel but I'm not going to. He probably already knows it and I *really* don't want him to *need* it.

I make sure to get to school early so I can drop the automaton into the Design and Technology Department for judging. The deadline is nine o'clock, since they're going to give the results in a brief assembly after lunch.

Interesting-looking things made from wood dot the DT lab—clearly most people didn't leave it this late to submit.

Thankfully I don't run into Shaun anywhere, and at lunch I go to join Daniel and Razim in the empty year group classroom, where Razim is frantically doing his Mathematics homework in between bites of his sandwich—Mathematics is our final lesson this afternoon and he's left it a bit late. Still, from the way he's flying through the work, it's not so serious a problem as it would have been for me. Engineer brain, definitely.

"Katie," says Daniel, when I arrive, "I don't know if you heard at Mass yesterday, but Father Thomas was finally able to announce it—youth group's resuming this week. With a bang! We're having a talk about Saint Andre Bessette. I thought you might be interested."

"Andre Bessette..." The name sounds familiar, though the rest of what Daniel said unleashes uneasy butterflies in my tummy. "He's got something to do with Saint Joseph..."

"Yeah, he was a Canadian, responsible for the building of one of the largest churches in North America..."

"...dedicated to Saint Joseph! I remember reading about him. He was in a religious order, wasn't he? Very humble, poor health, not much education, but everyone

78

came because when he prayed with them miracles happened."

"That's the guy. If you want to come, we're meeting in the presbytery garden and the church hall garden in two groups—no more than six in each—and the speaker—from Saint Andre's order—is going to sit on the wall in between so both groups can hear him."

I laugh. "Rule-of-six-compliant group meeting. That's clever."

"Oh, Father Thomas is ingenious."

I bite my lip, eyeing Daniel. "Do you always go to Mass on Sunday?"

Daniel looks startled. "Of course."

Of course. Hmm. And I was sitting there yesterday, doing my homework. Did I let Saint Joseph down again? "How…uh…important is it?"

Daniel's expression grows serious. "Well, very. The Church insists we go to Mass every Sunday because it's very important that at least once a week we don't let *anything* come between us and God, and that we meet as a community." He eyes me worriedly. "I saw you at Mass at Christmas. I assumed you just go at a different time than me?" I can hear the question in his voice.

"Mum stopped taking me to Mass after she divorced Dad," I say defensively.

"That's so sad. She is still welcome at Mass, you know."

"Yeah?" It comes out more challenging than I intended. "Can she receive communion?"

Daniel makes a face. "I couldn't say. She'd need to discuss it with Father Thomas. These things can get quite complicated."

"But, uh, what do you think?" I demand.

Daniel shrugs. "Well…if she went up, I doubt a priest would refuse her. But *should* she go up? Depends, doesn't it? Is she in a new relationship?"

What? Yuck. "No!"

"Was there…you know, abuse?"

"*No!*"

"And, uh, was the divorce, like, mutual?"

"No, Dad didn't want it. Despite…you know."

"Oh." Daniel looks solemn, then a little uncertain. "Well…I think that changes it rather. I think there's something called 'spousal abandonment' and that's really serious. But, heck, what do I know? She'd need to talk to Father Thomas, he'd know. But she can still go to Mass, either way. Both of you can."

"Yeah, well, I don't think she's gonna."

Daniel doesn't say anything. He just looks steadily at me. Heck!

"Okay, okay, I get it. I'm old enough to go on my own. I'll go in future."

Daniel beams so widely that I realize I *really* don't know enough about why Mass is important. Well, I'm sure he'll be happy to tell me sometime!

"Father Thomas will do confessions at the youth group," Daniel tells me, still looking as happy as though I've just been pulled from a burning building. "And my family goes to the eleven o'clock Mass on Sundays. Do you want a lift?"

Eleven. That's not horribly early. "What about germs? Won't your mum mind?"

Daniel flips a hand dismissively. "We're in the same school bubble, it's a very short drive, and we can open the windows. I think she'll be okay with it." He shoots me a sidelong look, mischief in his eyes. "Normally — non-Covid — it's a mortal sin to miss Sunday Mass, you know. Or rather — *it is if you know it is*." He waggles his hairless eyebrows at me. "And…oops — now you know!"

I throw my cereal bar in his general direction. "Oh, ha ha, *thanks*, Daniel."

He laughs, his eyes bright and alive in his pale face. For some reason my dream flashes into my mind, followed by two thoughts: first, that maybe getting fond of Daniel isn't a great idea.

Second, that it's already too late.

Before long, the four oldest year groups are filing into the school hall for the flash woodwork prize presentation, seated in our class bubbles. We're going to be having flash competitions all term, probably to try to make up for all the things cancelled in the last year. Of course, if it wasn't for Covid, we'd be too frantic revising for our exams to enter anything. I reckon having our teachers grading us is a lucky break for Daniel, who's missed even more school than the rest of us.

I glimpse Shaun with the oldest year, further down the tiered seating. He gives me such a black glare I know the letter arrived before he set off for school this morning. But there's a helpless edge to his rage. He knows he's lost his leverage on me and if he makes a nuisance of himself, Daniel has the video of what happened in the park.

Razim wanted Daniel to at the very least send that video to the headmistress in the hopes Shaun would get chucked off the rugby team, but Daniel just wants to forgive and forget. Though he did assure me that he has the video safe and I can have it if I need it. I know Shaun deserves it, after the way he's treated me, but I feel like I want to follow Daniel's example and forgive him, if I can manage it. If I don't let it go, he'll still have me prisoner.

As the headmistress and the head of DT come on stage to make the announcements Shaun shoots me another look, one of smoldering triumph. Guess he knows he's about to win and he's taking his satisfaction where he can. Who cares? It's just a little school competition, right? My dream was to build a working automaton, and I've achieved that.

A boy in Shaun's year gets announced as the third prize-winner. He stands up in his place for the applause while the head of DT displays his beautiful wooden sculpture from the stage like a shopping channel presenter.

"Second prize," says the headmistress, "goes to Shaun Mayock for his very fine tabletop bowling alley."

Shaun's shoulders go rigid. Beside Daniel, Razim bends over, clutching his stomach, shaking with laughter. I think Daniel's smiling under his mask, for all his determination to forgive and forget, and I struggle to keep a straight face. I dumped Shaun; it's over. I don't want us to be the two ex's who just can't stop sniping at each other.

"Second!" wheezes Razim. "He's so disappointed, the arrogant twerp, just look at him!"

Razim's giggles are becoming contagious. Shaun's disappointment is too poorly hidden and other people are starting to laugh too. Daniel elbows Razim in the ribs. *"Stop it!"*

Razim quiets down, and I'm grateful. If everyone around me laughs, I might as well have laughed out loud myself.

Fortunately the ripple of laughter subsides as Shaun

83

stands up, getting hold of himself, and smiles and nods with something approaching good grace.

Just the first-prize winner to be announced, and then it's time to hand in my Saint Joseph project in our next lesson. I think it's come out really well. Hopefully I'll get a good mark and it'll help my final grade. But I don't really care that much. Not when I've got a great spiritual father and powerful protector out of it, who's already fixed so much in my life. Shaun. My automaton. New friends when I never even realized I needed them. If only...*Dad*.

Don't get greedy, Katie, I tell myself.

"And first prize goes to this *outstanding, fully-working* automaton, 'The Carpenter and Child' by Katie Hayward, Razim Sadiq, and Daniel Whelkes."

My attention jerks back to the hall as my jaw drops open behind my facemask. *What?* But there's the automaton appearing from beneath the cloth as the head of DT unveils the winning entry.

"And before you all applaud," chips in the head of DT, sounding thoroughly over-excited, "I must ask you to stay quiet and listen while I demonstrate so you get the *full* effect!"

He takes hold of the little metal handle in the side of the mounting box and begins to turn it. It's a metal handle, not a wooden one, because Razim inserted a music box mechanism into the automaton, so now...

84

Not only does the carpenter's arm start going back and forth—*saw, saw*—but it does it to the tinny sounds of 'Amazing Grace.' After four turns the logs suddenly move forward on their ribbon, one of them seemingly dropping into the basket at the carpenter's feet (though of course the band has merely disappeared into the housing box to bring the log around again). And after six turns…little Jesus tugs on Joseph's cloak.

"That's adorable!" squeals a girl in the front row, who can see it properly.

Murmurs of "Cool!" "Wow…" and "I saw something like that once…" fill the hall.

"Er, why is my name on there?" mutters Razim, rising reluctantly as the headmistress urges the three of us to our feet.

Daniel's eyes are wide over his mask. "Well, you did make it work. But why is *my* name on there?"

"Probably because it was your music box that got cannibalized," Razim mutters back, and they shoot looks at me that hover between questioning and accusatory.

"I could hardly take all the credit!" I protest. "I'd have been handing in a box of loose parts without you two!"

Although, when I wrote their names down on the entry slip with my own, I certainly didn't imagine we'd be standing up together in front of everyone. Maybe

85

Saint Joseph isn't taking any chance of letting me slip back into those shallow, unhealthy friendships.

Right now, I really don't care.

CHAPTER 12

MONDAY

Mum is so pleased and proud when she hears our automaton won first prize that she orders in Chinese and we have a longer dinner than usual. I take advantage of her good mood to ask her if I can go to the youth group meeting on Thursday and when she hears it's at church she goes quiet for a while. But then she asks if social distancing guidelines will be followed and I explain about the groups of six and she says yes. Phew!

When I get up to my room I do my novena, then flop on the bed and stare at the ceiling. What a rollercoaster the last week has been! Hmm, when will theme parks re-open? I'm surprised just how relieved I feel, knowing I'm not going to be trying to stay in the cool set anymore, that I won't have to be constantly worrying about how every last little thing comes across.

I feel...free. Free to be me.

I can get Father Thomas to bless my Cord of Saint Joseph on Thursday. And I can confess about all those missed Masses. And about the stuff with Shaun. Oh yeah. I am so looking forward to confessing *that* and feeling...clean. And I want to hear more about one of Saint Joseph's biggest enthusiasts. Huh, look at me, so excited! If you'd told me a week ago I would be going to a church youth group meeting—let alone looking forward to it—I'd have thought you were mad...

"Excuse me?" Joseph catches a pigeon seller by the arm. "Have you seen a boy, looks very like my wife, about twelve?"

The man shakes his head, so we hurry on through the busy temple court. Three days we've been searching, ever since we realized that I'd thought Jesus was with the men's group in the pilgrim caravan, and Joseph had thought Jesus was with the women's group. We've searched all around the area of Jerusalem where we set up our booths for Passover and found nothing, but someone just told us they thought they saw a boy like Jesus up in the temple yesterday, so we've rushed up here...

"Excuse me, honored rabbi..." Joseph stops a Pharisee in a many-tasseled shawl. "Have you seen a boy, about twelve, who looks very like my wife?"

The Pharisee's attention flicks to my face and I cast my eyes down to avoid any unseemly eye contact.

"Are you His parents?" the Pharisee says. "He's been sitting under there for three days. Asks the most extraordinary questions and hasn't run out of them yet. The scribes and rabbis don't know what to do with Him."

We follow his gaze to the colonnade on the south side of the temple, where a larger than unusual knot of people gather around one of the teachers of the law.

"Thank you! Thank you so much!" Joseph dashes straight across the court—nothing is going to delay him now we're this close. Weaving among the people, I follow, and we wriggle our way through the crowd until we reach the centre.

An old rabbi sits on his stool in the shade, and at his feet Jesus sits cross-legged on His spread-out cloak, face tilted up at the elderly man as though drinking in his words.

"Jesus!"

"Jesus!"

We rush forward. I manage to enfold Him in my arms first, so Joseph wraps his arms around us both. Relief fills me so full I can barely breathe, though that may be partly the strength of Joseph's embrace.

"Jesus," I whisper, when I can finally speak again, "how could You do this to us? Your father and I have been going crazy with worry, searching for You!"

Jesus looks up at us calmly, not at all like a twelve-year-old who has been alone in a big city for three days and nights. Has He been right here in the temple the entire time? Why didn't we think to check here first!

"But Amma, did you not know I would be about My Heavenly Father's business?"

I have no reply to that. Joseph holds us even tighter, pressing a kiss onto Jesus's head. Tears of love glisten in his eyes, the intensity of his emotion naked in this moment of relief. A true father loves their child more than life—nothing could have kept Joseph from Jesus, even if he had to search all week without an hour's sleep or get past a legion of Roman soldiers.

But we've found Him. Our family is re-united.

Blessed be God.

The phone ringing downstairs jerks me awake. I blink at the ceiling. Did I fall asleep? How very... Daniel...of me. I'd better do some schoolwork. But I've only got as far as sitting up when I hear Mum calling.

"Katie? It's...it's for you..."

For me? Who would be calling the landline? I go out to the landing. She's standing at the foot of the stairs, holding the hands-free phone at arm's length like it's a snake she's thinking of stamping on.

"Who is it?"

Mum's lips tighten. Her thumb hovers over the button on the phone that will disconnect the call. But, finally, she thrusts it towards me.

"It's your father."

"What?" My shriek strangles itself in my throat and

I leap down the stairs, four at a time, then grab the handset from Mum. I raise it to my ear. I'm starting to shake. "D...Dad?"

There's a long silence. A swallowing sound. And a voice. My dad's voice. "K...Katie? Sw...sweetie?"

"Dad?"

"Katie..."

I turn around and sprint back up the stairs, the phone clamped to my ear.

"Dad?"

"Katie... Sweetie..." His voice sounds choked. I think he's crying.

Slamming my room door behind me, I throw myself on the bed, shaking more and more.

"Dad..." I just keep saying it, and he just keeps whispering, "Katie, sweetie," except when he can't seem to speak for several breaths at a time.

Tears are streaming down my face and I'm sniffing and sobbing.

"Dad..."

It's ages before we both calm down enough to say anything else. But when we do...

"Dad? Why...*why haven't you called me?* It's been *three years...*" Despite my joy, anger stirs.

"I'm sorry, sweetie. I'm *so, so* sorry. I was just so ashamed. I thought you'd be better off without me in your life. I thought you wouldn't *want* me in your life. I was just…I was so ashamed. But this week…I couldn't stop thinking about you. Worse than normal. And I began to think…well, I got talking with the prison chaplain and…and he convinced me I was being a fool. That it didn't matter what I'd done, you'd still want to hear from me. If that's wrong…then I'm sorry. I'll hang up; I'll never bother you again—"

"NO!" I clutch the phone as though it will stop him ending the call. "No! You're not wrong! I'm only angry you didn't call me *sooner*! I thought you didn't *care*, Dad! What else would I think?"

"I'm so sorry, Katie." His voice is wobbling, like he's crying again. He does care. It really was some other stupid reason why he didn't contact me sooner... "Katie, you can come and visit me." He blurts it out quickly, like he's afraid to hear my answer. "Will you?"

"Of course I will! You're my dad!"

He starts crying again, and so do I. My dad. It's really my dad. I've got him back at last.

Saint Joseph, thank you, thank you, thank you, thank you, thank you!

Oh, you said it, Mary: Blessed be God!

If you liked this book, please write a short review—a few lines are enough—and tell your friends about the book too.
Your support is important. Thank you.

SAINT JOSEPH: WHAT WE KNOW.

If someone reads even a selection of the suggested books and resources on Saint Joseph they will probably notice apparent contradictions in how Joseph's life is presented. For example, whether he was old or young when he married Mary. Whether he was a widower or a young virgin. And so on.

This is quite simply because what we know about Saint Joseph fills precisely 10 pages and if you turn to page 118 you can read through it in a couple of minutes. And even with the biblical account, the timeline can be interpreted in different ways. This is because Matthew and Luke both knew different facts and/or felt different things to be important and worth recording, with the result that a complete narrative has to be slotted together from both Matthew and Luke. In presenting such a synthesis I have used the order of events that has always seemed most plausible to me, and which I have most often seen presented, however, it should be noted that a few of the events, most significantly whether Mary told Joseph about her pregnancy before or after visiting Elizabeth, could quite legitimately be placed in a different order.

What does this mean for learning about Saint Joseph? It simply means that when dipping into resources on Saint Joseph it is worth keeping in mind that outside of the simple biblical facts, everything we 'know' about Saint Joseph comes from interpretation of the biblical texts, pious speculation, and (non-binding) private revelation. There are various, sometimes conflicting, traditions and the Church does not affirm any one over any other.

For example, Fr. Donald H. Calloway's book 'Consecration to St. Joseph: The Wonders of Our Spiritual Father' contains a host of interesting facts and stories about Saint Joseph and those who have been devoted to him—including an excellent (but, of course, arguable) section on why Saint Joseph was probably a young man—but is sometimes in danger of presenting Saint Joseph as some sort of demi-god, divorced from normal humanity and almost robotic in his perfection.

For example, Fr, Calloway pushes—arguably a little too strongly—the 'Reverence Theory,' which is the idea that Saint Joseph did not seek to divorce Mary—the word, according to the theory, has been mistranslated— but he only sought to send her away because, having mystical knowledge that what was happening inside her was holy and not something she bore blame for, he felt himself too unworthy to be near her. Many people would find this interpretation a stretch, since if Joseph had such mystical knowledge, why would the angel need to be sent to him? And how can his reverence for Mary and what was happening in her be squared with sending her away in a culture where single parenthood, especially for a woman, meant stigma and almost certain destitution? But, of course, the theory does have its supporters, Fr. Calloway and Dr. Mark Miravalle, and many other saints and scholars. The point is, so do the other theories.

In other words, when reading about Saint Joseph, one must simply be aware that there often isn't a 'correct' interpretation and if someone tries to tell you otherwise, whether in a book or in person, they are drifting off course. The main point about any theory about Saint Joseph and his life is to bring us closer to the saint. It's not about being right, only about building a relationship.

So dip into the fascinating range of resources, learn more about the times Saint Joseph lived in, the experiences people have had living under the shelter of his spiritual fatherhood, and the results of his powerful intercession. Above all, remember, Jesus gave us his mother as our spiritual mother—and he wants his adopted father to be our father too.

MORE INFORMATION

FICTION

The Staircase (Movie)
The full movie is available to view on YouTube
*Do Carpenters Dream of Wooden Sheep: St. Joseph's story
as dreamt by a sleeping teenage boy* – Corinna Turner
A Friends in High Places story that can be read as a
standalone or between books 1 and 2.

NON-FICTION

Patris Corde – Pope Francis
Apostolic Letter on the 150th Anniversary of the
Proclamation of Saint Joseph as Patron of the
Universal Church.
Saint Joseph Prayers and Devotions – Donal Anthony
Foley (Catholic Truth Society)
Saint Joseph: Help for Life's Emergencies – Kathryn J.
Hermes
Meet Your Spiritual Father – Dr. Mark Miravalle
Consecration to Saint Joseph – Fr. Donald H. Calloway

OTHER RESOURCES

Angelic Warfare Confraternity
www.angelicwarfareconfraternity.org

DISCUSSION QUESTIONS

1) *At the beginning of the book Katie is placing a lot of value on things like physical appearance, worldly achievements, and the approval of her peers.*

- Do you think she is right to value these things?
- Why/why not?
- How does Katie's idea of what is important change throughout the book?
- Do you think she is going to be happier as a result?

2) *Shaun tries to manipulate Katie without actually coming straight-out and making it clear he's blackmailing her.*

- Why is this sort of pressure harder to identify and resist?
- Is there any moral difference, in your opinion, between this and 'normal' blackmail?

3) *Even when Katie is fairly sure what Shaun is trying to do, the lack of certainty leaves her prone to attacks of guilt and doubt during which she questions her conclusions.*

- Why is it so important during these times that Katie talks to someone else about what is happening?
- Do you think Katie would have got free of Shaun so quickly if she hadn't told Daniel (and later her mum) what was happening?

- Why/Why not?

4) *The devil is a huge fan of the 'divide and conquer' tactic. He loves it when people bottle up their problems and keep them to themselves.*
- Have you ever had a problem that seemed huge until you discussed it with someone, after which it suddenly seemed much smaller and more manageable?
- Why do you think talking about problems with a trusted friend, family member, or safe pair of ears (counselor, teacher, youth group leader, priest, etc.) is so useful?

5) *Katie finds talking to Daniel about his potentially fatal illness incredibly difficult. It is clear Razim does too. Daniel's other friends find it so hard that they stay away from him entirely.*
- Have you ever talked to someone in a similar position?
- Did you find it difficult?
- Why/Why not?
- If you were in that position again, would you wish to be like Razim or like Daniel's other friends?
- Why/Why not?

6) *Katie finds the photo she sent to Shaun humiliating, even though at the time she took it she sees nothing wrong with wearing a strapless dress, which would be just as revealing.*
- What is the difference—if any—between wearing a towel in a photo like the one Katie took, and wearing a strapless dress to a party?
- Do you think it is dangerous to take and send a photo of that nature to someone else, even if you think you can trust them?
- Do you agree with Daniel's/Father Thomas' view that it should never be done?
- Why/Why not?

7) *Towards the end of the book Katie makes a commitment not to become intimate with a boyfriend before marriage. She finds this resolution profoundly liberating and empowering, allowing her to step outside the expectations of secular culture and take control.*
- Have you ever made such a resolution?
- Would you like to?
- Why/Why not?

8) *Katie marks her resolution by putting on the Cord of Saint Joseph. Although a physical sign (such as the Cord of Saint Joseph or enrolment in the Angelic Warfare*

Confraternity) is strictly optional when making such a commitment, it can be helpful.

- Why do you think this is so?
- Do you think you would find it helpful?
- Why/Why not?

9) *Katie's father betrayed his marriage vows to Katie's mother. He also stole a large amount of money from the company he was working for. Despite this, Katie suffers terribly from his absence and just wants him back.*

- Would you feel the same way?
- Why/Why not?
- Katie's father was sorry for what he had done and didn't want a divorce. How do you feel about the fact that Katie's mother insisted on one anyway?
- Why do you feel that way?

LITANY OF SAINT JOSEPH

Lord, have mercy on us.

Christ, have mercy on us.

Lord, have mercy on us. Christ, hear us.

Christ, graciously hear us.

God the Father of Heaven, *have mercy on us.*

God the Son, Redeemer of the world, *have mercy on us.*

God the Holy Ghost, *have mercy on us.*

Holy Trinity, One God, *have mercy on us.*

Holy Mary, *pray for us.*

Saint Joseph, *pray for us.*

Illustrious son of David, *pray for us.*

Light of patriarchs, *pray for us.*

Spouse of the Mother of God, *pray for us.*

Chaste guardian of the Virgin, *pray for us.*

Foster father of the Son of God, *pray for us.*

Watchful defender of Christ, *pray for us.*

Head of the Holy Family, *pray for us.*

Joseph most just, *pray for us.*

Joseph most chaste, *pray for us.*

Joseph most prudent, *pray for us.*

Joseph most valiant, *pray for us.*

Joseph most obedient, *pray for us.*

Joseph most faithful, *pray for us.*

Mirror of patience, *pray for us.*

Lover of poverty, *pray for us.*
Model of workmen, *pray for us.*
Glory of home life, *pray for us.*
Guardian of virgins, *pray for us.*
Pillar of families, *pray for us.*
Solace of the afflicted, *pray for us.*
Hope of the sick, *pray for us.*
Patron of the dying, *pray for us.*
Terror of demons, *pray for us.*
Protector of Holy Church, *pray for us.*

Lamb of God, Who takes away the sins of the world,
Spare us, O Lord!
Lamb of God, Who takes away the sins of the world,
Graciously hear us, O Lord!
Lamb of God, Who takes away the sins of the world,
Have mercy on us!
V. He made him the lord of His household,
R. *And prince over all His possessions.*

Let Us Pray
O God, Who in Thine ineffable Providence didst
vouchsafe to choose Blessed Joseph to be the spouse
of Thy most holy Mother, grant, we beseech Thee,
that he whom we venerate as our protector on earth
may be our intercessor in Heaven. Who lives and
reigns forever and ever. *Amen.*

ROSARY OF SAINT JOSEPH

ON THE CRUCIFIX

O Lord, in order to honor Saint Joseph as he deserves, Thou hast taken him body and soul to Heaven to Crown him with glory, thus signifying to the world, both visible and invisible, that Thou hast made Joseph Thy foster-father, the supreme steward of all Thy possessions.

LARGE BEADS

After saying the above prayer, skip to the large bead and say the following prayer, which will be said on each of the large beads.

We beseech Thee, O Lord, that we may find aid in the merits of the Spouse of Thy Most Holy Mother, so that what we cannot obtain by ourselves may be given us through his intercession, who livest and reignest with God the Father in the unity of the Holy Spirit, one God forever and ever. Amen.

SMALL BEADS

For each decade of small beads, it is customary to meditate on events in the life of Joseph.

1. *Betrothal to Mary (Mt 1:18).*
2. *Annunciation to Joseph (Mt 1:19-21).*
3. *Birth and Naming of Jesus (Mt 1:22-25).*

4. *Flight into Egypt (Mt 2:13-15).*

5. *Hidden Life at Nazareth (Mt 2:23; Lk 2:51-52).*

Other mysteries can be substituted, such as the "Finding of Jesus in the Temple," the "Death of Saint Joseph" and the "Coronation of Saint Joseph in Heaven."

On each small bead the following prayer is recited:

Hail Joseph, Son of David, thou whose holiness surpasses that of all Angels and Saints, blessed art thou amongst men, thou who wert chosen to be the Spouse of the Blessed Virgin Mary of whom was born Jesus. Glorious Saint Joseph, now reigning body and soul in Heaven, protector of the Universal Church, pray for us poor sinners now and at the hour of our death.

Amen.

Similar to the typical Rosary, each decade is completed with a *Glory Be.*

THE NOVENA OF THE HOLY CLOAK

Recited daily for 30 days.

In the name of the Father, and of the Son,
and of the Holy Spirit. *Amen.*
Jesus, Mary and Joseph,
I give Thee my heart and my soul.

(Recite the *Glory Be* 3 times to our Heavenly Father in
thanksgiving for having exalted St. Joseph to a
position of such exceptional dignity.)

OFFERING

I

O Glorious Patriarch St. Joseph, I humbly prostrate
myself before Thee. I beg the Lord Jesus, thine
Immaculate Spouse, the Blessed Virgin Mary, and all
the Angels and Saints in the Heavenly Court, to join
me in this devotion. I offer thee this precious cloak,
while pledging my sincerest faith and devotion. I
promise to do all in my power to honor thee
throughout my lifetime to prove my love for thee.

Help me, St. Joseph. Assist me now and throughout
my lifetime, but especially at the moment of my
death, as thou wert assisted by Jesus and Mary, that I
may join thee one day in Heaven and there honor
thee for all eternity. Amen.

II

O Glorious Patriarch St. Joseph, prostrate, before thee and thy Divine Son, Jesus, I offer thee, with heartfelt devotion, this precious treasury of prayers, being ever mindful of the numerous virtues which adorned thy sacred person. In thee, O Glorious Patriarch, was fulfilled the dream of thy precursor the first Joseph, who indeed seemed to have been sent by God to prepare the way for thy presence on this Earth. In fact, not only wert thou surrounded by the shining splendor of the rays of the Divine Sun, Jesus, but thou wert splendidly reflected in the brilliant light of the mystic moon, the Blessed Virgin Mary. O Glorious Patriarch, if the example of the ancient Jacob, who personally went to congratulate his favorite son, who was exalted on the throne of Egypt, served to bring all his progeny there, should not the example of Jesus and Mary, who honored thee with their greatest respect and trust, serve to bring me, thy devoted servant, to present thee with this precious cloak in thy honor.

Grant, O Great St. Joseph, that the Almighty God may turn a benevolent glance toward me. As the ancient Joseph did not reject his guilty and cruel brothers, but rather accepted them with love and protected and saved them from hunger and death, I beseech thee, O

Glorious Patriarch, through thine intercession, grant that the Lord may never abandon me in this exiled valley of sorrows. Grant that He may always number me as one of thy devoted servants who dost live serenely under the patronage of thy Holy Cloak. Grant that I may live always within the protection of this patronage, every day of my life and particularly at that moment when I draw my dying breath.

PRAYERS

I

Hail O Glorious St. Joseph, thou who art entrusted with the priceless treasures of Heaven and Earth and foster-father of Him Who doth nourish all the creatures of the universe. Thou art, after Mary, the Saint most worthy of our love and devotion. Thou alone, above all the Saints, wert chosen for that supreme honor of rearing, guiding, nourishing and even embracing the Messiah, Whom so many kings and prophets would have so desired to behold.

St. Joseph, save my soul and obtain for me from the Divine Mercy of God that petition for which I humbly pray. And for the Holy Souls in Purgatory, grant a great comfort from their pain.

(Recite the *Glory Be* 3 times to our Heavenly Father in

thanksgiving for having exalted St. Joseph to a
position of such exceptional dignity.)

II

O powerful St. Joseph, thou wert proclaimed the
Patron of the Universal Church, therefore, I invoke
thee, above all the other Saints, as the greatest
protector of the afflicted, and I offer countless
blessings to thy most generous heart, always ready to
help in any need.

To thee, O Glorious St. Joseph, come the widows, the
orphans, the abandoned, the afflicted, the oppressed.
There is no sorrow, heartache or anguish which thou
hast not consoled. Deign, I beseech thee, to use on my
behalf those gifts which God hast given thee, until I
too shall be granted the answer to my petition And
thou, Holy Souls in Purgatory, pray to St. Joseph for
me.

(Recite the *Glory Be* 3 times to our Heavenly Father in
thanksgiving for having exalted St. Joseph to a
position of such exceptional dignity.)

III

Countless are those who have prayed to thee before
me and have received comfort and peace, graces and
favors. My heart, so sad and sorrowful, cannot find

rest in the midst of this trial which besets me. O Glorious St. Joseph, thou knowest all my needs even before I set them forth in prayer. Thou knowest how important this petition is for me. I prostrate myself before thee as I sigh under the heavy weight of the problem which confronts me.

There is no human heart in which I can confide my sorrow; and even if I should find a compassionate creature who would be willing to assist me, still he would be unable to help me. Only thou can help me in my sorrow, St. Joseph, and I beg thee to hear my plea.

Has not St. Teresa left it written in her dialogues that the world may always know "Whatever you ask of St. Joseph, you shall receive."

O St. Joseph, comforter of the afflicted, have pity on my sorrow and pity on those Poor Souls who place so much hope in their prayers to thee.

(Recite the *Glory Be* 3 times to our Heavenly Father in thanksgiving for having exalted St. Joseph to a position of such exceptional dignity.)

IV

O Sublime Patriarch St. Joseph, because of thy perfect obedience to God, thou mayest intercede for me.

For thy holy life full of grace and merit, hear my prayer.

For thy most sweet name, help me. For your most holy tears, comfort me.

For thy seven sorrows, intercede for me. For your seven joys, console me.

From all harm of body and soul, deliver me. From all danger and disaster, save me.

Assist me with thy powerful intercession and seek for me, through thy power and mercy, all that is necessary for my salvation and particularly the favor of which I now stand in such great need.

(Recite the *Glory Be* 3 times to our Heavenly Father in thanksgiving for having exalted St. Joseph to a position of such exceptional dignity.)

V

O Glorious St. Joseph, countless are the graces and favors which thou hast obtained for afflicted souls. Illness of every nature, those who are oppressed, persecuted, betrayed, bereft of all human comfort, even those in need of their life bread — all who imploreth thy powerful intercession are comforted in their affliction.

Do not permit, O dearest St. Joseph, that I alone be the

only one of all who hast appealed to thee, to be denied this petition which I so earnestly beg of thee. Show thy kindness and generosity even to me, that I may cry out in thanksgiving, "Eternal glory to our Holy Patriarch St. Joseph, my great protector on Earth and the defender of the Holy Souls in Purgatory."

(Recite the *Glory Be* 3 times to our Heavenly Father in thanksgiving for having exalted St. Joseph to a position of such exceptional dignity.)

VI

Eternal Father, Who art in Heaven, through the merits of Jesus and Mary, I beg Thee to grant my petition. In the name of Jesus and Mary I prostrate myself before Thy Divine presence and I beseech Thee to accept my hopeful plea to persevere in my prayers that I may be numbered among the throngs of those who live under the patronage of St. Joseph.

Extend Thy blessing on this precious treasury of prayers which I today offer to him as a pledge of my devotion.

(Recite the *Glory Be* 3 times to our Heavenly Father in thanksgiving for having exalted St. Joseph to a position of such exceptional dignity.)

CLOSING PRAYER OF THE HOLY CLOAK

O Glorious Patriarch St. Joseph, thou who wert chosen by God above all men to be the earthly head of the most holy of families, I beseech thee to accept me within the folds of thy holy cloak, that thou mayest become the guardian and custodian of my soul.

From this moment on, I choose thee as my father, my protector, my counselor, my patron and I beseech thee to place in thy custody my body, my soul, all that I am, all that I possess, my life and my death.

Look upon me as one of thy children; defend me from the treachery of my enemies, invisible or otherwise, assist me at all times in all my necessities; console me in the bitterness of my life, and especially at the hour of my death. Say but one word for me to the Divine Redeemer Whom thou wert deemed worthy to hold in thine arms, and to the Blessed Virgin Mary, thy most chaste spouse. Request for me those blessings which will lead me to salvation. Include me amongst those who art most dear to thee and I shall set forth to prove myself worthy of thy special patronage.

Amen.

PRAYER TO SAINT JOSEPH SLEEPING

Oh Saint Joseph,
You are a man greatly favored by the Most High.
The angel of the Lord appeared to you in dreams,
while you slept, to warn you and guide you
as you cared for the Holy Family.
You were both silent and strong, a loyal and
courageous protector.
Dear Saint Joseph,
as you rest in the Lord, confident of His absolute
power and goodness, look upon me. Please take
my need…

*(mention your request here and place it under a statue or
beneath an image of Saint Joseph sleeping)*

…into your heart, dream of it, and present it to
your Son. Help me then, good Saint Joseph,
to hear the voice of God, to arise, and act
with love. I praise and thank God with joy.
Saint Joseph, I love you.
Amen.

THE CORD OF SAINT JOSEPH

400 years ago in Antwerp, Belgium, an Augustinian nun called Sister Elizabeth was sick and doctors thought her likely to die. Since she had a special devotion to Saint Joseph, she had a cord be blessed in his honor, which she then wrapped around her waist. After a few days, her pain disappeared while she was praying for Saint Joseph's intercession. Her case was accessed by multiple doctors—including a Protestant doctor—who proclaimed her cure to be miraculous.

When, 200 years later, the miracle was publicized—particularly in Verona, Italy—this devotional cord was adopted by a hospital in Verona in March of 1842 and distributed to its patients. Then, on September 19, 1859, the devotion of Saint Joseph's cord was officially adopted. A blessing formula was created, indulgences were added by Pope Pius IX, and widespread private use permitted.

The White Cord of Saint Joseph can be used not only as a remedy against physical illness, but also as a powerful support in living the virtues of chastity and purity of heart.

Graces Associated with the Cord

There are 5 primary graces attached to wearing the cord and reciting the corresponding prayers with faith:

1. Saint Joseph's special protection
2. Purity of soul
3. The grace of chastity
4. Final perseverance
5. Particular assistance at the hour of death

The Practical Commitment

You can make your own cord or buy one readymade. It should be made of thread or cotton, finishing at one end with seven knots, representing the Seven Joys and Sorrows of Saint Joseph. It can be worn as a girdle for purity or chastity and humility, or around the shoulders for obedience. You should get it blessed by a priest with the faculties for this blessing. Pius IX approved a special formula for the blessing of this cord.

The Spiritual Commitment

The daily commitment associated with the devotion is to pray seven *Glory Be's* along with the following prayer to Saint Joseph for Purity:

O GUARDIAN of Virgins and holy Father Saint Joseph,
into whose faithful keeping were entrusted
Christ Jesus, Innocence Itself, and
Mary, Virgin of virgins,
I pray and beseech thee by these dear pledges,
Jesus and Mary, that,
being preserved from all uncleanness,
I may with spotless mind,
pure heart and chaste body,
ever serve Jesus and Mary most chastely
all the days of my life.
Amen.

Meditating on Saint Joseph's Seven Joys and Sorrows is also encouraged (see the final prayer).

Here are a few short petitions also associated with the cord:

Saint Joseph, model of those who love the Sacred Heart of Jesus, pray for us.

Saint Joseph, foster father of our Lord, Jesus Christ, and the spouse of Mary, pray for us.

Grant O holy Joseph, that, ever under your protection, we may pass our lives without sin. Amen.

THE SEVEN SORROWS AND SEVEN JOYS OF SAINT JOSEPH

Meditate on each and then say an
Our Father . . . Hail Mary . . . Glory be . . .

JOSEPH'S SEVEN SORROWS

1. The doubt of Saint Joseph *(Matt. 1:19)*
2. The poverty of Jesus' birth *(Luke 2:7)*
3. The Circumcision *(Luke 2:21)*
4. The prophecy of Simeon *(Luke 2:34)*
5. The flight into Egypt *(Matt. 2:14)*
6. The return from Egypt *(Matt. 2:22)*
6. The loss of the Child Jesus *(Luke 2:45)*

JOSEPH'S SEVEN JOYS

1. The message of the Angel *(Matt. 1:20)*
2. The birth of the Savior *(Luke 2:10-11)*
3. The Holy Name of Jesus *(Matt. 1:25)*
4. The effects of the Redemption *(Luke 2:38)*
5. The overthrow of the idols of Egypt *(Is. 19:1)*
6. Life with Jesus and Mary at Nazareth *(Luke 2:39)*
7. The finding of the Child Jesus in the Temple *(Luke 2:46)*

THE COMPLETE SCRIPTURAL ACCOUNT

A Synthesis of *Matthew* and Luke

The Angel Gabriel was sent by God, to a city of Galilee named Nazareth, to a virgin betrothed to a man whose name was Joseph, of the house of David; and the name of the virgin was Mary. And upon entering, the Angel said to her: "Hail, full of grace. The Lord is with you. Blessed are you among women." And when she heard this, she was disturbed by his words, and she wondered what kind of greeting this might be.

And the Angel said to her: "Do not be afraid, Mary, for you have found favor with God. Behold, you shall conceive in your womb, and you shall bear a son, and you shall call his name: JESUS. He will be great, and he will be called the Son of the Most High, and the Lord God will give him the throne of David his father. And he will reign in the house of Jacob for eternity. And his kingdom shall have no end."

Then Mary said to the Angel, "How shall this be done, since I am a virgin?"

And in response, the Angel said to her: "The Holy Spirit will pass over you, and the power of the Most High will overshadow you. And because of this the Holy One who will be born of you shall be called the Son of God. And behold, your cousin Elizabeth has herself also conceived a son, in her old age. And this is the sixth month for her who is called barren. For no word will be impossible with God."

Then Mary said: "Behold, I am the handmaid of the Lord. Let it be done to me according to your word."

And the Angel departed from her.

And in those days, Mary, rising up, traveled quickly into the hill country, to a city of Judah. And she entered the house of Zechariah, and she greeted Elizabeth. And it happened that, as Elizabeth heard the greeting of Mary, the infant leaped in her womb, and Elizabeth was filled with the Holy Spirit.

And she cried out with a loud voice and said: "Blessed are you among women, and blessed is the fruit of your womb. Why should I be honored by a visit from the mother of my Lord? For behold, as the voice of your greeting came to my ears, the infant in my womb leaped for joy. And blessed are you who believed, for the things that were spoken to you by the Lord shall be accomplished."

And Mary said: "My soul magnifies the Lord.

And my spirit leaps for joy in God my Savior.

For he has looked with favor on the humility of his handmaid.

For behold, from this time, all generations shall call me blessed.

For he who is great has done great things for me, and holy is his name.

And his mercy is from generation to generations for

those who fear him.

He has accomplished powerful deeds with his arm.

He has scattered the arrogant in the intentions of their heart.

He has deposed the powerful from their seat,
and he has exalted the humble.

He has filled the hungry with good things,
and the rich he has sent away empty.

He has taken up his servant Israel, mindful of his mercy,

just as he spoke to our fathers:

to Abraham and to his offspring forever."

Then Mary stayed with her for about three months. And she returned to her own house. *Mary had been betrothed to Joseph, but before they lived together, she was found to have conceived in her womb by the Holy Spirit.*

Then Joseph, her husband, since he was just and did not want to expose her publically, decided to divorce her quietly. But just when he had resolved to do this, behold, an Angel of the Lord appeared to him in his sleep, saying:

"Joseph, son of David, do not be afraid to accept Mary into your home as your wife. For what has been formed in her is of the Holy Spirit. And she shall give birth to a son. And you shall call his name JESUS. For he shall accomplish the salvation of his people from their sins."

Now all this occurred in order to fulfill what was spoken by the Lord through the prophet, saying:

"Behold, a virgin shall conceive in her womb,

and she shall give birth to a son.
And they shall call his name Emmanuel,
which means: God is with us."
Then Joseph, when he woke up, did just as the Angel of
the Lord had instructed him, and he took her into his home as
his wife.

And it happened in those days that a decree went out from Caesar Augustus, for the whole world to be enrolled. This was the first enrollment; it was made by the ruler of Syria, Quirinius. And all went to be registered, each one to his own hometown.

So Joseph set out from Nazareth in Galilee and traveled to Judea, to the city of David, which is called Bethlehem, because he was of the house and family of David, in order to be registered, together with Mary his espoused wife, who *though Joseph knew her not,* was with child. Then it happened that, while they were there, the time came for her to have her child. And she brought forth her firstborn son. And she wrapped him in swaddling clothes and laid him in a manger, because there was no room for them at the inn.

And there were shepherds in the same region, being vigilant and keeping watch in the night over their flock. And behold, an Angel of the Lord stood near them, and the brightness of God shone around them, and they were struck with a great fear.

And the Angel said to them: "Do not be afraid. For,

behold, I proclaim to you a great joy, which will be for all the people. For today a Savior has been born for you in the city of David: he is Christ the Lord. And this will be a sign for you: you will find the infant wrapped in swaddling clothes and lying in a manger."

And suddenly there was with the Angel a multitude of the celestial army, praising God and saying,

"Glory to God in the highest, and on earth peace to men of good will."

And when the Angels had departed from them into heaven, the shepherds said to one another, "Let us cross over to Bethlehem and see this word, which has happened, which the Lord has revealed to us."

And they went quickly. And they found Mary and Joseph; and the infant was lying in a manger.

Then, upon seeing this, they understood the word that had been spoken to them about this boy. And all who heard it were amazed by this, and by those things which were told to them by the shepherds. But Mary treasured all these things, pondering them in her heart.

And the shepherds returned, glorifying and praising God for all the things that they had heard and seen, just as it was told to them.

And after eight days were ended, and the boy was to be circumcised, they gave him the name JESUS, the name given by the Angel before he was conceived in the womb.

And after the days of her purification were fulfilled, according to the law of Moses, they brought him to Jerusalem, in order to present him to the Lord, just as it is written in the law of the Lord, "For every male opening the womb shall be called holy to the Lord," and in order to offer a sacrifice, according to what is said in the law of the Lord, "a pair of turtledoves or two young pigeons."

And behold, there was a man in Jerusalem, whose name was Simeon, and this man was just and God-fearing, awaiting the consolation of Israel. And the Holy Spirit was with him. And he had received an answer from the Holy Spirit: that he would not see his own death before he had seen the Christ of the Lord. And prompted by the Spirit, he went to the temple. And when the child Jesus was brought in by his parents, in order to act on his behalf according to the custom of the law,

Simeon also took him up, into his arms, and he blessed God and said:

"Now you may dismiss your servant in peace,
O Lord, according to your word.
For my eyes have seen your salvation,
which you have prepared before the face of all peoples:
the light of revelation to the nations
and the glory of your people Israel."
And as his father and mother wondered over these

things which were spoken about him, Simeon blessed them, and said to his mother Mary: "Behold, this one is destined for the ruin and for the rising of many in Israel, and as a sign which will be contradicted. And a sword will pass through your own soul, so that the thoughts of many hearts may be revealed."

And there was a prophetess, Anna, a daughter of Phanuel, from the tribe of Asher. She was very advanced in years, and she had lived with her husband for seven years from her virginity, before becoming a widow. She was eighty-four years old and never left the temple. She was a servant to fasting and prayer, night and day. And entering at the same hour, she began to praise the Lord. And she spoke about him to all who were awaiting the redemption of Israel.

And after they had performed all things according to the law of the Lord, *behold, wise men from the east arrived in Jerusalem, saying: "Where is he who was born king of the Jews? For we have seen his star in the east, and we have come to worship him."*

Now King Herod, hearing this, was disturbed, and all Jerusalem with him. And gathering together all the leaders of the priests, and the scribes of the people, he consulted with them as to where the Christ would be born. And they said to him: "In Bethlehem of Judea. For so it has been written by the prophet:

'And you, Bethlehem, in the land of Judah,
are by no means least among the leaders of Judah.

For from you shall go forth the ruler
who shall guide my people Israel.' "

Then Herod, secretly calling the Magi, learned from them
the exact time when the star appeared to them. And sending
them to Bethlehem, he said: "Go and diligently ask questions
about the boy. And when you have found him, report back to
me, so that I, too, may come and adore him."

And when they had heard the king, they went away. And
behold, the star that they had seen in the east went before
them, until it stood still above the place where the child was.

Then, seeing the star, they were gladdened by a very
great joy. And entering the home, they found the boy with his
mother Mary. And so, falling prostrate, they adored him. And
opening their treasures, they offered him gifts: gold,
frankincense, and myrrh. And having been warned in a
dream that they should not return to Herod, they went back
by another way to their own region.

And after they had gone away, behold, an Angel of the
Lord appeared in sleep to Joseph, saying: "Rise up, and take
the boy and his mother, and flee into Egypt. And remain there
until I tell you. For Herod intends to seek the boy to destroy
him."

And getting up, Joseph took the boy and his mother by
night, and left for Egypt. And he remained there, until the
death of Herod, in order to fulfill what was spoken by the Lord
through the prophet, saying:

"Out of Egypt, I called my son."

Then Herod, seeing that he had been fooled by the Magi,

was very angry. And so he gave orders to kill all the boys who were in Bethlehem, and in all its borders, from two years of age and under, according to the time that he had learned by questioning the Magi.

Then what was spoken through the prophet Jeremiah was fulfilled, saying:

"A voice has been heard in Ramah,

great weeping and wailing:

Rachel crying for her sons.

And she was not willing to be consoled,

because they were no more."

Then, when Herod died, behold, an Angel of the Lord appeared in sleep to Joseph in Egypt, saying: "Get up, and take the boy and his mother, and return to the land of Israel. For those who were seeking the life of the boy are dead."

And rising up, he took the boy and his mother, and he went into the land of Israel. But, hearing that Archelaus reigned in Judea in place of his father Herod, he was afraid to go there. And being warned in a dream, he withdrew into parts of Galilee. And arriving, he lived in a city which is called Nazareth, in order to fulfill what was spoken through the prophets:

"For he shall be called a Nazarene."

Now the child grew, and he was strengthened with the fullness of wisdom. And the grace of God was in him. And his parents went every year to Jerusalem, at the time of the solemnity of Passover.

When he was twelve years old, they went up to

Jerusalem, according to the custom of the feast day. And when the feast was over and they were on their way home, the boy Jesus remained in Jerusalem. But his parents did not realize this. Supposing that he was in the group, they went a day's journey, before seeking him among their relatives and acquaintances. And not finding him, they returned to Jerusalem, seeking him.

And it happened that, after three days, they found him in the temple, sitting in the midst of the doctors, listening to them and questioning them. But all who listened to him were astonished over his prudence and his responses. And upon seeing him, they were overcome. And his mother said to him: "Son, why have you acted this way toward us? Behold, your father and I were searching for you in great anxiety."

And he said to them: "How is it that you were seeking me? For did you not know that it is necessary for me to be about my Father's business?"

And they did not understand what he meant.

And he went down with them and came to Nazareth. And he was subordinate to them. And his mother stored up all these things in her heart. And Jesus advanced in wisdom, and in age, and in grace, with God and men.

DON'T MISS

DO CARPENTERS DREAM OF WOODEN SHEEP?

THE STORY OF SAINT JOSEPH—WITH A SCI-FI TWIST!

Razim's staying overnight to help his friend Daniel, who's sick with leukaemia, but he's forgotten his phone! Lying awake after watching Bladerunner, Razim reads the only story he can find—about Joseph and Mary—only to fall asleep and find himself in futuristic Merillia.

In Merillia, his name is Cleopas, and his big brother, Jo, is considering an arranged marriage to a girl called Miryam. Soon, events are in motion that will change their lives—and the world—forever.

For anyone who feels over-familiar with the Holy Family's story after Christmas after Christmas of nativity plays, this imaginative re-telling thoroughly blows the dust off.

A standalone spin-off from Corinna Turner's 'Friends in High Places' series, it can be read on its own or in between books 1 and 2.

TURN OVER TO READ THE FIRST 2 CHAPTERS!

If you haven't read book 1 in the series,
why not pick up THE BOY WHO KNEW *today?*

"You have leukemia."

Daniel's just received the worst news a teen can get. The adults in his life are crumbling under the shock. In desperation, he turns to his parish priest for help and is introduced to a boy his age, Carlo Acutis—who just happens to be dead.

Daniel's convinced the priest is wasting his time. But as he struggles to come to terms with his uncertain future an unlikely friendship develops between him and the holy dead boy—who may not be quite so dead after all.

DO CARPENTERS DREAM OF WOODEN SHEEP?

CHAPTER 1: BEDTIME READING

"Oh…" Swearing under my breath, I fish around in my overnight bag, even though I have a crystal-clear memory of plugging the charger into my phone and leaving it on my window ledge at home. No phone for me tonight.

I wasn't very loud, but over on the bed, Daniel stirs slightly. "What's wrong, Razim?"

I stop rummaging in my bag and lie still on my wobbly camp bed, not wanting to disturb him. "Oh, nothing."

Daniel's particularly tired tonight and he doesn't press the issue. I hear his breathing deepen and slow as he falls asleep, but I don't feel sleepy yet. I should, 'cos I was here Monday night and I'll be here again next Monday and I can't believe how tiring it is having even two disrupted nights a week. But that's why I'm here, of course.

When Daniel had his first round of chemo his parents insisted on one of them staying with him in his room every night, in case he needed anything. Daniel swore—still does—that he doesn't need it, but after the morning when they found vomit in a lot of places it shouldn't be, and Daniel curled up freezing-cold in the middle of the floor halfway to the bathroom because he'd got too tired to crawl back into bed, they insisted.

But they were like zombies by the end and that really upset Daniel. So when his second round of chemo clashed with another Covid lockdown, I hatched a clever plan. Well, I thought so at the time. I could come and stay over two nights a week to give his mum and dad a break. And that way I'd get to see Daniel, despite the lockdown, because I'd count as a 'carer.'

It took a lot of persuading, with both sets of parents—we coaxed, we argued, we even begged—and then to my shame, I almost quit after the first time. I suppose I had this idea that we'd chat and have at least a bit of fun. I guess I wasn't really prepared for all the—

Over on the bed, Daniel stirs, making a slight retching sound. I leap up from the camp bed, grab the basin from the floor and hold it out. "Need this?"

"Ugh..."

Yep, he vomits.

"You done?" I ask at last, trying, as usual, to sound as though holding a basin of puke is no biggie.

"Think so." His head sinks towards his pajama sleeve so I put the bowl down quick, snatch a tissue and hastily wipe his chin. I've learned all sorts of little tricks for keeping the smell down. He's so pale, the brown skin of my hand contrasts sharply with his face. Coffee and Cream, my big brother Sayeed used to call us—and not in a nice way—but when he saw Daniel after his first round of chemo he called us Coffee and Milksop. I pushed him over into a bush but then I couldn't run for it the way I usually would because Daniel wasn't up to it, so I got well-pounded. Daniel said I shouldn't have reacted but he also gave me a tissue for my nose so I forgave him.

"You gonna need this again, man?" I nod to the bowl.

Daniel shakes his head without lifting it. "Don't see how I can possibly have any more where that came from," he jokes weakly.

Too right. It's been particularly bad, tonight. We tried to watch *Bladerunner* after I arrived—well, after I'd showered and put on clean clothes to reduce the risk of transmitting anything to immune-suppressed Daniel— but Daniel puked through most of it. Ugh, he's sixteen, not much older than me, he shouldn't be this sick!

I barely managed to make myself come back, the second time, it was all such a shock. The vomiting. The stench. And just...seeing Daniel this weak and down. Unbearable. But I figured I wasn't much of a friend if I could let a bit of puke stop me helping out, and I *made* myself come back. And I'm glad. I mean, he's my best mate, but if he can't beat this leukemia, well, he could just be...gone...by the time this Covid-thing is all over.

"You're nearly done with the chemo, right?" I say,

when his eyes don't close again immediately. "There're what, less than two weeks left?" Like we don't both know that, but it's the most cheerful thing I can think to say.

"Yep." He musters a smile.

Even with his weird new optimism about everything, a few times he's got so tired that he's just cried. Quiet, helpless weeping, like he simply can't help it. It's horrible. And I can tell he's ashamed when he gets like that, so I just talk cheerful, like crying's no big deal, and try to distract him from how awful he's feeling, but I don't feel like it works. Thankfully, he's not quite that tired tonight. Yet.

"And the Lockdown's easing on twenty-ninth March," I say. "So, just think, a few days to get your strength back, and we can go down to the park, get an ice cream, fly my hovercraft..." I got a remote-controlled hovercraft for Christmas, and Daniel hasn't had much chance to see it in action, yet. It knocks the socks off a remote control car or boat, the way it can just go straight down the bank and out onto the lake.

Daniel nods and smiles. "Well, if it's actually still in one piece!"

I laugh. "Yeah, okay, I pulled it apart and changed a few things, but I got it back together okay."

"Of course you did," murmurs Daniel. But then his smile fades. His hand rises to run over his bald head.

"Wish it wasn't getting so hot—" He breaks off suddenly, his pale cheeks going slightly pink, the way they do when he feels like he's been grumbling. The new Daniel doesn't hold with grumbling.

I guess he's worried he won't want to wear a woolly hat, the way he did after his last course of treatment. I remember after his hair started falling out again, all couple of millimeters of it, how he just muttered, "Here we go again," and never said another word about it. I guess it bothers him more than he likes to let on.

"Ah, we'll be, like, a skinhead gang, man. It'll be cool."

Daniel shoots me a look, smiles a too-polite smile and closes his eyes.

Okay, that went down like a lead balloon. Guess you can't really have a skinhead 'gang' when only one of you is bald. I carry the stinking basin to the bathroom, empty it and rinse it out, getting it back to the room as fast as I can, just in case—but Daniel's sleeping quietly.

At least it sounds like the doctors are hopeful hitting it again this soon will put it into remission. They didn't really give him long enough to recover in between, but they said this was the only chance.

It will be worth it. If...

I sigh, stretch out on my cot, fold my arms behind my head and stare up at the ceiling. Tired or not, it's too early to sleep. I can't believe I forgot my phone. I'm an idiot.

I glance around the room. Beside Daniel's computer stands a pile of schoolbooks that he still tries to open occasionally because he doesn't want to get held back a year. No, thanks. I glance at the bedside table. Bible...nope, some sort of prayer book, er, nope...what's that one? I sit up and pick up a thin booklet and look at the cover. A handsome young man stands protectively over a beautiful young woman holding a baby. All with a similar brown skin tone to mine. I eye their features, trying to figure out what race they are, but I'm not sure. Something Middle Eastern, perhaps? Their noses are quite sharp.

The Tale of Joseph and Mary, says the heading. Hey, maybe it's fiction. That'd do. As long as it's not a romance. But Daniel's not into soppy stuff and it must be quite a manly romance, from the cover. I flop back on the camp bed and open the booklet.

Oh. Maybe it's not fiction. There's an 'introduction' by someone or other. I flick past it. Uh-oh. The first chapter begins with a Bible quote. Heck, it's another of Daniel's religious books, isn't it? He went super-religious after getting his diagnosis. It makes me kinda want to ditch him sometimes, when he really gets going, but even if we hadn't been friends since kindergarten, that light in his eye... It's scary as heck, but it fascinates me, too. I just wish I could figure out how he can be so flaming *happy* when he's in this fix.

I don't want to start rootling around the room for something else to read and wake Daniel, so I scan the quote. Okay, nothing terrifying. It just says something about 'a virgin engaged to a man whose name was Joseph, of the house of David. The virgin's name was Mary.' Guess that's Mary and Joseph on the cover.

Hang on...I turn the booklet over and read the back. Oh, okay. So this is about Maryam, mother of Jesus, or Isa as my parents would call him. And Joseph is her *husband*? I might have heard something about a Joseph, at Christmas time, but the penny hadn't dropped. Maryam was *married*? Wow. What sort of man would put up with his wife just getting mystically pregnant like that? I mean, *back then*? When I was little and my parents still took us to the mosque occasionally and even made us sit in some classes, I don't remember ever hearing about Joseph. What sort of man could be worthy to marry Maryam, Isa's *ammi*?

I turn back to the beginning and start reading. The story is way more exciting than I expected. Soon I'm well impressed with this Joseph guy. Maryam was lucky to have him. Except I guess Daniel would say it wasn't luck, right?

When, yawning, I put the booklet down rather later than I intended and plonk my head on the pillow,

135

Joseph still strides through my mind, young and brave and reminding me a heck of a lot of Daniel—at least, the way he is now. That bewildering trust that I can't quite figure out. That freakish calm. Sounds like Joseph had it too.

I don't really have any problems in my life—may have thought I did once, but Daniel's illness has made it clear I don't have any real ones—but if I ever had problems like those characters in *Bladerunner*, or like Joseph and Maryam, or like Daniel...it would be nice to be all brave and peaceful. But how do they do it?

Yeah... Another yawn stretches my jaws. Be nice... But how...?

+

RAZIM'S DREAM

CHAPTER 2: THE BETROTHAL

"I can't believe you're going through with this." I raise my voice over the sound of a hover-bus passing too close over the top of our ancient domestic pod.

Jo carefully straightens the colorful wide sash that's been part of Merillian formal wear for centuries, even though it's falling out of use in favor of Imperial fashions, nowadays. "Why? It's traditional."

"Yeah, but you don't have to anymore. That's a freedom

the Empire actually has brought."

Jo shoots me a look of amusement. "It's an arranged marriage, little bro, not a forced marriage. Big diff. And it's not like the way it used to be done. All we're doing today is getting introduced. Then we get to know each other, and only then do we decide whether we want to go ahead and get married."

"I still don't see why you don't just find a girl for yourself."

"Because the matchmaker has spent decades learning who's likely to be compatible with whom. So I might as well give this a try first, right?"

When he puts it like that, it doesn't sound so dumb, not if you're looking for marriage and no sordid messing around, which is definitely what my big brother is after. Some people use the info-xchange to find girlfriends, after all. Probably better to trust your future happiness to a person than to a machine.

"Well, I've got your back, whatever you decide."

He grins at me. "Thanks, Cleo." He fidgets with his sash again. He's more nervous than he's letting on.

"You look good," I tell him. "She'll swoon."

"Ah, very funny." But he looks fractionally more relaxed as he heads for the broken up-down conveyer. Not for the first time, as we trek downstairs, I wonder what it's like to live in a domestic pod where everything works. Jo swears that when I was very young, when Amma and Abba were both still alive and had recently moved here from Bethlasa, our pod was all in proper order, like other people's. But I don't remember. I barely even remember them. Jo's been keeping us with his woodcarving since forever.

At least now I'm old enough to have my hover-permit, I can do delivery work and make some money too. Seeing that I'm rubbish at carving. I'm good at fixing things, but you have to be careful, showing serious skills. Imperial soldiers get a bounty for every conscript they sign up, which is why they get so rough about it — but if they sign up someone skilled, they get double. They don't need carpenters — wood goods are for decoration — but engineers? I'm better off delivering stuff, even if the pay is low.

Sealing the pod behind us, we climb into the hover-van I managed to scrape together enough to buy and we're off through the streets to the matchmaker's.

"Okay," I say, parking two doors down, under a lurid flickering neon sign. "Time to meet your fate."

"Very funny," says Jo. Sweating. Well, he decided to do this.

We keep a careful lookout for swipe-thieves, regional security forces, or imperial soldiers as we walk the short distance to the matchmaker's door. The first will beat you and take your valuables, the second will frisk you in a more official manner but make your stuff disappear just as fast, and the third might do either — or worse, conscript you on the spot.

In we go. The up-down here works, and soon we're being shown into the matchmaker's receiving room. Oh boy...the prospective bride is already here, standing between her elderly parents with her head bowed. They look old enough to drop off their perches any time, in fact. Is that why she's put herself up for an arranged marriage? If they've got nothing to leave her...well, it's hard for a woman to survive alone. Between Imperial taxes and the Regional Supreme Leader's whims and the dangerous streets... Well, that doesn't matter, if she's both nice and pretty. I guess Jo, being Jo, will only really care if she's nice. But I stare, trying to make out her face.

Jo stops and bows formally, so I do the same. Our traditions are getting forgotten fast, now we're part of the Empire, but not by Jo.

The bridal party bows as well, and finally the young woman looks up. Girl. The girl looks up. She's young, maybe sixteen, about my age, her skin smooth coffee perfection, her eyes dark and warm. And her poise...like a katachara dancer. And...and...something else about her. What is it?

Jo is staring at her as though he's been struck dumb, but the matchmaker is clearly used to this and begins some spiel of introduction that gives Jo time to pull himself together. Then I take tea with the matchmaker and the elderly parents of the bride—Joachim and Annei—while Jo goes into the matching chamber for private refreshments with the girl herself. Miryam, her name is. Her parents are sweet and kind and doddery, and embarrassingly enthusiastic about me—

139

even though it's Jo who's going to be marrying their daughter if it all works out—and I'm not sorry when the hour is up.

Jo is silent as we take the up-down back to the lobby. It's up to me to keep an eye out for danger as we walk the short distance back to the hover-van. He settles into the seat silently, still staring into space.

"So?" Once my door is sealed to keep out the smog, I can't wait any longer. "What did you think of her?"

He turns his head slowly, like a man coming out of a dream, wonder in his eyes. "Did you ever…ever see anything so pure in all your life? Anyone so pure…"

Pure. Yes, that was it, the indefinable quality about Miryam. Purity. Not unlike my big brother, only—and I'd not have thought it possible—even more so. I glance at Jo's face. Oh yeah, it's a done deal, all right.

And three weeks later, Miryam and Jo become formally betrothed. Big surprise. Not.

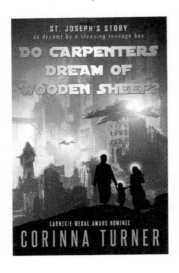

I AM MARGARET

**IN MARGO'S WORLD,
THE 'IMPERFECT' ARE RECYCLED.
LITERALLY.**

Margaret Verrall dreams of marrying the boy she loves and spending her life with him. But she's part of the underground network of Believers – and that carries the death penalty. But before she can be unmasked as a Believer, she fails her Sorting and is reassigned as spare parts. Bane swears to rescue her before she can be dismantled, but a chance to take on the system ups the stakes beyond mere survival. Now she has to break out of the Facility—or face the worst punishment of all: Conscious Dismantlement.

If you enjoy books like THE HUNGER GAMES, UNWIND, or NEVER LET ME GO but wish they had that inspirational edge, I AM MARGARET is the book you've been waiting for! This page-turner combines adventure and suspense with a touch of romance, and delves into the real emotional cost of martyrdom and standing up for what you believe.

READ ON FOR A SNEAK PEEK!

I AM MARGARET SNEAK PEEK

We filed into the gym when it was all over, sitting on benches along the wall. Bane guided Jonathan Revan to a free spot over on the boys' side. In the hall through the double doors the rest of the school fidgeted and chatted. Once the end of semester assembly was over, they were free for four whole weeks.

Free. Would I ever be free again?

I'd soon know. One of the inspectors was wedging the doors open as the headmaster took his place on the stage. His voice echoed into the gym. "And now we must congratulate our New Adults! Put your hands together, everyone!"

Dutiful clapping from the hall. Doctor Vidran stood by the door, clipboard in hand, and began to read names. A boy. A girl. A boy. A girl. Sorry, a young man, a young woman. Each New Adult got up and went through to take their seat in the hall. Was there a pattern...? No, randomized. Impossible to know if they'd passed your name or not.

My stomach churned wildly now. Swallowing hard, I stared across the gym at Bane. Jonathan sat beside him, looking cool as a cucumber, if a little determinedly so. *He* wasn't in any suspense. Bane stared back at me, his face grim and his eyes fierce. I drank in the harsh lines of his face, trying to carve every beloved detail into my mind.

"They might call my name," Caroline was whispering to Harriet. "They might. It's still possible. Still possible..."

Over half the class had gone through.

Still possible, still possible, they might, they might call my name... My mind took up Caroline's litany, and

142

my desperate longing came close to an *ache.*

"Blake Marsden."

A knot of anxiety inside me loosened abruptly—immediately replaced by a more selfish pain. Bane glared at Doctor Vidran and didn't move from his seat. Red-faced, the deputy headmistress murmured in Doctor Vidran's ear.

Doctor Vidran looked exasperated. "Blake Marsden, known as Bane Marsden."

Clearly the best Bane was going to get. He gripped Jonathan's shoulder and muttered something, probably *bye.* Jonathan found Bane's hand and squeezed and said something back. Something like *thanks for everything.*

Bane shrugged this off and got up as the impatient inspectors approached him. *No...don't go, please...* Yes! He was heading straight for me—but the inspectors cut him off.

"Come on...Bane, is it? *Congratulations,* through you go..." Bane resisted being herded and the inspector's voice took on a definite warning note. "Now, you're an adult, it's your big day, don't spoil it."

"I just want to speak to..."

They caught his arms. He wrenched, trying to pull free, but they were strong men and there were two of them.

"You *know* no contact is allowed at this point. I'm sure your girlfriend will be through in a moment."

"Fiancée," snarled Bane, and warmth exploded in my stomach, chasing a little of the chill fear from my body. He'd read my story already.

"*If,* of course, your *fiancée,*" Doctor Vidran sneered the un-PC word from over by the door, "is a perfect specimen. If not, you're better off without her, *aren't* you?"

Bane's nostrils flared, his jaw went rigid and his

knuckles clenched until I thought his bones would pop from his skin. Shoulders shaking, he allowed the inspectors to bundle him across the gym towards Doctor Vidran. *Uh oh...*

But by the time they reached the doors he'd got sufficient hold of himself he just stopped and looked back at me instead of driving his fist into Doctor Vidran's smug face. He seemed a long way away. But he'd never been going to reach me, had he?

"Love you..." he mouthed.

"Love you..." I mouthed back, my throat too tight for actual words.

Then a third inspector joined the other two and they shoved him through into the hall. And he was gone.

Gone. I might never see him again. I swallowed hard and clenched my fists, fighting a foolish frantic urge to rush across the gym after him.

"*Really,*" one inspector was tutting, "we don't usually have to drag them *that* way!"

"Going to end up on a gurney, that one," apologized the deputy headmistress, "So sorry about that..."

Doctor Vidran dismissed Bane with a wave of his pen and went on with the list.

"They might..." whispered Caroline, "they might..."

They might...they might...I might be joining Bane. I might... Please...

But they didn't. Doctor Vidran stopped reading, straightened the pages on his clipboard and glanced at the other inspectors. "Take them away," he ordered.

AVAILABLE NOW
in paperback and eBook!

ACKNOWLEDGEMENTS

I'd like to thank Lisa Theus, Sr. Teresa Cardinez, OP, and Leslea Wahl for all their excellent editorial help, and Sr. M. Catherine Bloom, OP, for the beautiful cover illustration.

Thanks to my parents for all their support, and to my Mum for her honest critiques.

And not forgetting Saint Joseph the Carpenter, the patron of this book—and last but the opposite of least, the Holy Spirit, who is responsible for it all.

ABOUT THE AUTHOR

Corinna Turner has been writing since she was fourteen and likes strong protagonists with plenty of integrity. She has an MA in English from Oxford University but has foolishly gone on to work with both children and animals! Juggling work with the disabled and being a midwife to sheep, she spends as much time as she can in a little hut at the bottom of the garden, writing.

She is a Catholic Christian with roots in the Methodist and Anglican churches. A keen cinemagoer, she lives in the UK. She used to have a Giant Snail called Peter with a 6½" long shell, but now makes do with a cactus and a campervan!

Sign up for **free short stories** & **news** at:
www.UnSeenBooks.com

Get in touch with Corinna:
Facebook: Corinna Turner - Twitter: @CorinnaTAuthor

Made in the USA
Monee, IL
29 July 2021

74535638R00090